ALSO BY P.K. NORTON

Avenging Madonna

Amy Lynch rustles up a brand-new mystery…and learns that knowledge of local history can be worth its weight in gold.

The crime of cattle rustling didn't die with the old west. It's alive and well at the Madonna Inn and Ranch in San Luis Obispo, California. The Madonna family isn't a bit happy about it. Neither is New England Casualty & Indemnity, the company which insures the Madonnas.

Insurance investigator Amy Lynch heads west to assess the situation. She becomes acquainted with two of the Madonna cowhands—Gus, who is recently deceased under questionable circumstances and Lance, who is handsome and dashing—and very much alive.

Amy learns the ins and outs of cattle ranching, as well as the local legends dating back to the days of the gold rush. The plot thickens rapidly and the body count increases, nearly including Amy herself.

I'll admit I've fallen hard for insurance investigator Amy Lynch, heroine of the entertaining series by mystery writer PK Norton! Amy is an endearing character whose previous adventures have kept readers, including me, wanting more. Now in Norton's sixth novel in the series, Avenging Madonna, *Amy is sent to solve a cow rustling muystery out west and plenty of fun and danger ensues. It's no wonder more readers are smitten by Amy,. She makes it easy!"*

—Jordan Rich, WBZ Boston / iHeart Media

"Glimpses of San Luis Obispo's past add interest to a unique tale."

—Kirkus Reviews

Deadly Diamonds

Are diamonds really a girl's best friend? Are they actually forever? And what is causing the sudden epidemic of diamond jewelry disappearing from households across Massachusetts? Insurance investigator Amy Lynch sets out to answer this question when theft claims at New England Casualty and Indemnity take an alarming upturn. What she discovers about the NEC&I agents who insure these diamonds takes her down a dark and disturbing road—a road from which she almost fails to return.

Norton's latest installment in her Amy Lynch Investigation series features accessible prose and likable characters, and it benefits from the fact that mysteries set in the insurance industry are relatively rare. The story opens strongly, with a stealth murder from the perspective of the killer, and Norton flows easily from that point ... A novel with appealing characters and a good setup

—Kirkus Reviews

PK Norton is back with another finely cut mystery! It's Amy Lynch at her best, investigating a rash of diamond robberies...Murder is in the air and Amy is in a race to solve the crime before she, too, becomes a victim. One cannot help but admire Amy as we stay up late reading to find out how she will go about cracking another beguiling case. She is resourceful, smart and just the kind of woman all of us want to root for.

—Jordan Rich,
WBZ Boston, iHeart media

Direct Elimination

There is no such thing as a coincidence. Or is there? Are random occurrences which take place at the same time, or in the same location, totally unrelated events? Or do they converge in time and space in order to right a wrong or put the universe back on track?

In other words, is there a connection between the dead fencer found by firefighters in Andy Yesley's cellar and the 20-year-old baby's skeleton also discovered there?

This is what insurance investigator Amy Lynch must determine as she delves into the fallout from what at first appears to be an ordinary fire loss.

"It's a story that has a tragic beginning and a bittersweet ending. Leave it to Norton, who spent her entire career in the insurance industry, to make investigating claims seem exciting, a formidable task ... This fast-moving mystery injects thrills and sizzle into claims settlement."

—Kirkus Reviews

Deep Secrets

Dead men tell no tales. Is that why Tom Griffin is lying near death in a Cape Cod hospital? Because of what he could reveal about Waltower—a top secret government project underway at Woods Hole Oceanographic Institute?

That's what Amy Lynch aims to learn. As an investigator for New England Casualty and Indemnity, Amy's job is to look into the supposed accident that put Tom into a coma. Amy has a personal stake as well. Tom Griffin is an old friend. Her first love. She struggles to keep her emotions in check as she seeks to discover what really happened to Tom. And why.

Amy fights her way through the sand-bagging she receives from WHOI. They say the project is need-to-know. Well, Amy needs to know. And the clearer the situation becomes to her, the greater the threat to her safety.

Will she uncover the truth in time to save herself from the same fate as Tom?

"If you love reading solid mysteries with a heroine you can identify with, then look no further than novelist P.K. Norton. Deep Secrets is her latest installment featuring intrepid insurance investigator Amy Lynch. Amy is no ordinary sleuth and the mystery set in and around Cape Cod will keep you guessing to the end!"

—Jordan Rich
WBZ iHeart Radio

"Norton draws on her experience working in the insurance industry to good effect in this latest series outing ... [she] manages to make insurance-related details as compelling as evidence collection in a conventional murder mystery. The plot is well-paced ... the characters are well-drawn. An entertaining, well-plotted mystery that offers good characterization and unexpected twists and turns."

—Kirkus Reviews

Dead Drop

Does the past ever really leave us? Not in Amy Lynch's world.

What starts out to be a well-deserved vacation for Amy—volunteering at an archaeological dig on the outskirts of Paris—turns ugly when the head archaeologist is found dead at the dig-site. A recently-uncovered relic from World War II threatens to expose treachery and betrayal from the time of the German Occupation. It endangers the life of anybody bold enough to delve into its significance.

New England Casualty and Indemnity, the insurance company where Amy works as a claims investigator, is insuring the dig. Amy's world turns upside-down as she reverts from vacation mode to conduct a full-blown investigation. She meets with obstacles, resistance and threats to her own safety—as well as an adorable French detective—in her quest to unmask a traitor.

"Norton has created an engaging protagonist in Amy, who is bright, brave, and tenacious. The tale features a small cast of characters, as many players disappear shortly after being introduced, so Amy has to carry the narrative load. Fortunately, she's up to the challenge; readers should quickly get involved in what happens to the feisty, heady heroine. With a neat twist in her fast-paced narrative, the author illustrates how events from 80 years in the past can affect people in the present, even Amy herself. Norton seamlessly blends history and mystery into a spellbinding thriller. This sequel accomplishes the unlikely feat of making an insurance investigator enthralling."

—Kirkus Reviews

Sweet Dreams, Sweet Death

Everybody loves Chef Garcia's key lime coconut petit fours. Some even say they're to die for. When four guests die at a wedding at the Beaux Rêves Hotel, the famous petit fours are blamed.

Insurance investigator Amy Lynch flies to Key West to prepare for a wrongful death suit. Her investigation is beset with problems. Hotel management pushes for a quick settlement regardless of fault. Local police call it a tragic accident. Potential witnesses are missing, deceased, or unhelpful. Amy fends off pressures from all sides and encounters death everywhere. The health inspector dies in an accident; the local reporter turns up drowned; a homeless woman Amy befriends is found dead. And deceased wildlife crosses her path more than once.

As she forges on in the face of these obstacles, Amy wonders if Key West is the tropical paradise of the travel brochures or a petri dish of death.

"Norton weaves realistic professional procedure and unexpected emotional jolts into the otherwise erotic flavor of Key West, creating a debut that will seriously contend for all the 'Best First' awards."

—Author Jeremiah Healy

"An impressively crafted and unfailingly entertaining novel by a master of the genre, Sweet Dreams, Sweet Death by P.K.
Norton is the first volume in what promises to be a simply out-standing new series starring Amy Lynch, female investigator."

—James A. Cox
Editor-in-Chief, Midwest Book Review

The Back of Beyond

An Amy Lynch Investigation

P.K. Norton

Names: Norton, P. K., author.
Title: The back of beyond / P.K. Norton.
Description: First Stillwater River Publications edition. | West
Warwick, RI, USA : Stillwater River
Publications, [2024] | Series: An Amy Lynch investigation
Identifiers: ISBN: 978-1-963296-11-2 (paperback)
Subjects: LCSH: Women insurance investigators--Tennessee--
Fiction. | Life insurance claims--
Tennessee--Fiction. | Truck drivers--Tennessee--Fiction. |
Cemeteries--Tennessee--Fiction. |
Bombs--Tennessee--Fiction. | LCGFT: Detective and mystery
fiction. | Thrillers (Fiction)
Classification: LCC: PS3614.O78266 B33 2024 | DDC: 813/.6--
dc23

Dedication

For Tom, with thanks for the cover design
as well as for his always-helpful input on the story.

And, as always, for Jack, for inspiring and encouraging me to
begin this journey.

The Back of Beyond

Chapter 1

Hog Jaw, Tennessee

Lillie checked her watch again—for the twentieth time in as many minutes. Nearly 11:00 P.M.. Jake should have been back by now. Something wasn't right.

They had argued before he left. About anything and everything, and sometimes nothing. Loudly and angrily. That was happening more and more lately. Jake was constantly pissing and moaning about something or other, and more than happy to air his grievances with Lillie. It wasn't good, not good at all.

Jake was still pleasant and reasonable with the guests. Lillie was grateful for that much. Times were tough. They couldn't afford to lose any business simply because the two of them weren't getting along.

This evening had been somewhat of an exception. They were getting along just fine, watching a movie together. Then a call had come in about an hour ago. From room 8. The guest told Jake he was concerned about a noise he heard outside his room. He wanted Jake to check it out. Lillie and Jake had heard the noise as well, but assumed it was from a large semi backfiring on the nearby interstate. That happened all the time. And sounds tended to be magnified at night.

Nevertheless, Jake was happy to oblige, as he always was. Only this time, he insisted on bringing his gun.

"What in hell for?" Lillie had asked him. "In all the years we've been here, running this damn motel, there's never been a problem. This town is quiet as a mouse, particularly after dark. And safe as well. You know that."

Jake shook his head. "I can't argue about the past. But things are different now. Times are changing. A body can't be too careful."

Lillie disagreed. "I think you're being ridiculous. Things are the same as they've always been around here—and probably always will be. Places like Hog Jaw never change. They're dead quiet and boring, day and night, year after year. Until we all die of boredom."

Jake's back stiffened. "That's not so," he said. "Things have changed. Business is up. We're getting more and more truckers all the time. But that may not be a good thing. Not all of these guys are the knights of the highway like they used to be. Some of them strike me as suspicious. Really, Lillie, who knows what they're really hauling in those rigs?"

Lillie sighed. "We can't think that way. The truckers are our life blood. We'd be hurting big time without their regular business."

"Maybe," Jake said. "Maybe not. This place survived just fine for years before the interstate was built. And nowadays it's not just the truckers we need to worry about, you know. It's those damn bikers, too. Things haven't been the same since they started coming around. They're loud and disruptive. Not the kind of business we're looking for. They're probably scaring away the better business, families and what-not."

"Give me a break, Jake. The bikers are just a bunch of middle-aged guys having a little fun on the weekends. They don't mean any harm. And they pay in cash. But go ahead and bring the damn gun if it makes you feel better."

"It will." Jake stomped across the office to the cabinet in the back where they kept the gun. Then he stood there and stared. "What the hell, Lillie? Where did you put the gun?"

"I didn't touch the damn thing. I never do, never have, never will. You ought to know that by now. Guns terrify me."

"Well somebody must have touched it. Because it isn't here."

"You probably moved it somewhere yourself," Lillie said.

"No way. This is where I keep it, and now it's gone. So what do you have to say about that?" He favored her with an unpleasant sneer.

She scowled back at him. "I say that maybe you better worry about the blasted gun another time and get out there right now to see what the guest in room 8 needs. We have to keep them all happy."

Jake slammed the door on his way out.

That was over an hour ago. Lillie had heard nothing from him. Something wasn't right.

She walked over to the front desk and checked the guest register. Lou Bancroft was in room 8. She knew him pretty well. He was a frequent guest at the motel. A long-haul trucker, his route brought him through the area at least once or twice a week. Lou was a large, burly, take-no-prisoners type of guy. A noise in the night seemed unlikely to alarm him. And he could certainly tell the difference between a vehicle back-firing and a more ominous sound. What in the world could the man have heard that alarmed him so?

And why wasn't Jake back by now?

Lillie's hands trembled as she checked her watch again. Then she knew she couldn't just sit and wait any longer. She grabbed her master keys, her phone and a flashlight. Not even taking the time to leave a note on the door in case anybody came by looking for a room, she locked the office and headed out to look for her husband.

The night was dark and moonless, the air still heavy from the heat of the day. The breeze from the direction of the interstate carried with it the ever-present stink of diesel exhaust. The song from a nearby night bird caused Lillie to jump. She sucked in her breath and marched down the row of rooms toward number 8, at the far end of the small motel. The light outside the room was unlit. Was that deliberate or had a bulb blown? She peered into the window to the room. Even with the curtain closed, it was obvious there was no light inside either. That made no sense. Where was Jake?

Lillie knocked on the door. "Hello? Anybody in there?" No response. She banged more insistently. "Is everything all right?" Still no response. That was not a good sign.

Lillie thrust the key into the lock and shoved the door open. She switched on the light, then froze at the sight which greeted her inside the room.

Lou Bancroft was across the room, slumped down on the floor with his back against the wall. His head hung loosely toward his chest, his eyes staring at nothing, his mouth open wide. A streak of blood stained the wall behind him.

She looked to her left. Her husband was on the floor by the bed, lying on his back, his eyes open wide. There was a small red hole in his forehead, a puddle of blood on the carpet beneath his head. He had a gun in his hand.

Lillie let out one large shriek, then collapsed onto the floor.

Chapter 2

Some people hate Monday mornings. Luckily, I've never been one of them. Mondays are usually when my boss Mark has a new and interesting—and occasionally exciting—assignment for me. As I climbed the stairs to his office on the third floor—aka Executive Heaven—I couldn't help but hope that today would be one of those days. Life had been quiet lately. I was ready for a new adventure.

I knocked lightly on Mark's office door.

"Come on in, Amy," he called to me. His desk was covered with manila file folders, his in-box piled high with unopened mail. No matter how advanced technology had become, the insurance business still managed to create a massive amount of paperwork. I rather liked the look. It made it appear as if Mark was truly involved in the everyday running of the company. And the technophobe in me felt like I had found a kindred soul. I liked paper.

Mark looked up at me and smiled. "Good morning. Please have a seat. Did you have a nice weekend?"

I plopped myself into his visitor's chair. "There's no such thing as a bad weekend. You know that. So what's up?"

"How would you like to take a road trip? A new claim just came in. I'd like you to head up the investigation."

"I guess that depends," I told him without a moment of hesitation.

"On what?" he asked.

"On where and when. Not to mention why." I was always comfortable speaking my mind with Mark. Besides being president and CEO of New England Casualty and Indemnity, and my boss, he was also the husband of my best friend Nancy. That meant he cut me a bit more slack than he did the other employees at NEC&I. I was grateful for that.

Mark leaned across his desk and folded his hands, but didn't look me in the eye. "The when is tomorrow. Sorry about the short notice. It can't be helped. This is important."

That was not what I hoped to hear. "Can it wait a few days? I'm supposed to meet Nancy for lunch on Wednesday. I haven't seen her in ages. Haven't seen my godchild either."

Mark shook his head. "Sorry, Amy. No can do. We need to jump on this loss right away, and with both feet."

That was either a very good sign or a very bad one. A sense of urgency about a loss often meant there was something interesting going on, something out of the ordinary in the world of insurance. Either way, it kept my job from becoming boring. I was grateful for that.

"And what about the where?" I asked.

Mark stared at his computer screen. "Hog Jaw, Tennessee."

I sat up straight. "Was it my imagination, or did you actually just say Hog Jaw, Tennessee? Is that even a real place?"

"I'm afraid so. It's a small town in the rural western part of the state."

"But why in hell is it named Hog Jaw?" I asked, then immediately regretted it. I wasn't sure I wanted to hear the story behind a name like that.

Mark shrugged. "Beats me. Towns do seem to have some oddball names out there, though. There's a place called Mouse Tail Landing. And another named Bucksnort. My favorite, though, is Mimosa. That sounds pleasant." He turned his computer screen so I could see a map of Tennessee, and pointed out the aforementioned towns for me.

So far I was less than thrilled. I was more of a city person. "Honestly, Mark, If I'm going to go to Tennessee, why couldn't the loss be in Nashville? Or Memphis? Someplace cool and interesting. If that map is accurate, Hog Jaw looks like it's in the middle of nowhere."

Mark opened a file on his desk. "That's not far from the truth. Hog Jaw is a tiny little oasis just off the interstate. It consists of an eight-room motel, a diner and a combination gas station / convenience store."

"It sounds more like a truck stop than a town," I told him. And I was pretty sure I wasn't going to like it there. Truck stops weren't my idea of a good time. I kept that to myself, at least for the time being.

Mark laughed at that, but didn't contradict it. "The entire place is well-maintained and apparently busy enough to stay in business, but it's also old and somewhat lonesome looking."

"You almost sound as if you've seen this so-called town in person."

"I have," he admitted. "And quite deliberately so."

Now that was a surprise. The Mark I knew and loved tended to prefer the urban scene.

My first question was: "How in the world did an international company like NEC&I end up insuring anything in a tiny little town in West Tennessee anyway?"

"Do you remember when Dick Mayfield in the sales department got married a couple years ago?"

I nodded.

"His bride was from Tennessee. He wrote the coverage on Hog Jaw as a favor to a relative of hers, a second cousin or some such thing, who was closing his insurance office and looking to help his clients replace their coverage elsewhere."

"My other question is: Why were you there?" I asked. "It sure doesn't sound like much of a vacation spot to me."

"But Nashville is," Mark replied. "A couple of years ago, Nancy and I spent a long weekend there. One of her favorite country singers was appearing at the Grand Ole Opry and we were lucky enough to get tickets. Dick had just written the Hog Jaw account. The description in the file intrigued me. I decided to check it out for myself as long as I was in the neighborhood."

At least that made some sense. Nancy was a big country music fan. "So tell me, exactly what does NEC&I insure in the town of Hog Jaw?" I asked. *And this ought to be interesting.*

"The entire town," Mark told me. "The motel, the diner and the gas station / convenience store. That's all there is. And it's all owned by a single family."

That struck me as odd, perhaps even mildly intriguing. "Okay. I'm with you so far. What type of loss are we looking at?"

"There are actually two separate losses, most likely related," Mark told me, a grim look passing over his face.

"And they are?"

"Damage to one of the motel rooms." He sucked in a breath and paused for a moment. "And untimely death."

My mouth fell open. No words came out.

Mark responded to the question in my eyes. "Besides insuring the entire town, we also wrote a life insurance policy on Jake Taylor, the motel owner. His body was found in one of the guest rooms last Thursday night. He and another man were both shot to death." Mark scanned the paper file on his desk. "The damage to the room is actually minimal - mostly blood stains on the carpet and the wall. As well as a few bullet holes in the wall and some of the furniture."

I shuddered as I pictured the scene. "Not your usual small-town loss."

"That's for sure," Mark said. "But I'm quite certain you'll be able to sort it all out with your usual aplomb."

I bounced what I'd just learned around in my head for a moment. "You know, despite the gruesome cause of both of these claims, in the end, they both are pretty cut and dried."

"What do you mean?" he asked.

"I mean … the property loss is fairly simple. We clean up the blood stains. Repaint the walls, clean or replace the carpet, repair or replace the damaged furniture. Probably just a few thousand dollars."

Mark nodded, but said nothing, waiting for me to finish.

"As for the death," I continued, "it is certainly unpleasant and un-timely, but, in the end, life insurance is pretty simple. Someone dies. We write a check."

Mark nodded again.

"So why send me?" I asked. "There must be some complication here that I'm not seeing."

"It's the life insurance policy," he said. "It was written less than six months ago, in the amount of $500,000."

"Who's the recipient?"

"The wife."

That wasn't surprising. "Are you telling me there's a reason we may not end up paying out on this policy? Like perhaps the widow did it?"

Mark shook his head. "It's not that. You know we couldn't deny her coverage unless she was actually convicted of killing her husband."

"Then what is it?"

"It's the suicide clause."

Aha! "Was it a suicide?"

Mark frowned. "We don't know. The local law enforcement folks are dragging their feet on making that determination."

"Do you know the cause of this foot-dragging?" I asked.

He nodded. "There were two bodies, both shot to death. Each body was holding a gun. Both guns had been fired. The forensic folks are trying to piece together what actually happened. I thought you might enjoy helping them out with that. When the cause of death is in question, it doesn't hurt for NEC&I to have somebody on the scene."

"So the question becomes: was our insured's cause of death murder or suicide? And the answer to that is worth $500,000 to NEC&I, or to the widow. This could turn out to be an interesting challenge," I said. "I guess I'm going to Hog Jaw."

Mark gave me a sly grin. "Please plan on arriving there tomorrow. I'm sure you'll do a wonderful job."

As I rose to leave his office, Mark added, "Oh, and by the way, please be on your very best professional behavior down there."

The remark hurt a little. "Do you mean as opposed to being my usual unseemly, lackadaisical and ill-behaved self?"

"I'm serious, Amy. Also, don't spend any more time than necessary. This incident got national attention over the weekend. Newspapers, online and TV news, you name it, they aired it. We can cash in on that if we play it right. We want to solve the case and settle the claim in record time. A little positive national attention never hurts. I'm sure you'll do us proud."

And perhaps have less fun in the process. Oh well. I was definitely up to the challenge.

Chapter 3

Monday 9:00 AM

I arrived back in my office on the first floor just as my assistant, good friend and occasional dog-sitter Peggy breezed through the door. She brushed her mop of unruly red curls away from her eyes and greeted me with her usual morning smile. "Sorry I'm late, Amy" she said breathlessly. "I overslept just a bit."

"Do I want to know why?" I asked.

"Probably not." She blushed slightly as she said this.

I pretended not to notice.

I filled her in on our new claim, and my impending departure for rural Tennessee. As usual, she was happy to sit for my dog Sam while I was gone. That always made my life a bit easier.

Peggy began clicking away on her computer. Then she let out a giggle.

"What's funny?" I asked.

"Would you believe there are at least three towns in the U.S. named Hog Jaw? There's yours in Tennessee, another in Arkansas and a third in Alabama."

"I'm not sure what that says about this great country of ours," I told her. "Maybe not so sure I want to know."

Peggy continued typing at warp speed.

"There's also a southern rock band by the same name. Who knew?"

"And how am I going to get to Hog Jaw, Tennessee?" I asked.

"Flying into Nashville looks like your best bet," she told me. "There's a 9:15 flight tomorrow morning."

"Sounds good." I could get up early if I had to.

Avoiding my eyes, Peggy asked, "Will that be one ticket or two?"

I chose to play dumb. "What do you mean?"

"Just wondering if perhaps Pete might be joining you."

Peggy and I had worked together for ages and knew each other well. She didn't let me get away with much. Sometimes I felt she was lucky I liked her. This was one of those times. I didn't answer her question.

"Oh, come on, Amy. This is me you're talking to. Don't you think it's time you and Pete moved past that incident in California? Nothing ever came of it. And Pete is too good a guy to lose. In your heart, you know that."

She was right. Pete had been the man in my life for a few years now. We were good together. Really good. Or at least we had been until last fall. I was on a case in San Luis Obispo and became enamored of a smoking hot cowboy named Lance. I came perilously close to succumbing to his many charms. A surprise visit from Pete eliminated the need for me to make that decision. Then, when Pete and Lance worked together to save my life, the attraction between me and Lance became obvious to Pete. Not to mention painful for him.

Since then, our relationship had been on shaky ground. We had never exactly severed communications, but neither did we sit down together and talk through our problems. That was more my fault than his. I tended to avoid unpleasant issues whenever possible. I loved Pete. There was no question about that. But I was nowhere near ready to settle down to a quiet life in the small town where he now lived. Or to face certain truths about my character. I kept telling myself I did not have commitment issues. I may have been lying about that.

Pete and I got together occasionally over the last next few months. It was awkward, and far from intimate, but we weren't quite ready to call it quits forever. He may or may not have had an affair a few months ago. I suspected it was so, but couldn't bring myself to ask. We'd been working on moving on lately, spending a lot more time together, good time, but were not quite there yet.

Pete had often accompanied me on out-of-state investigations in the past. We made a pretty good team. The lawyer in him added a helpful dimension to my job as a claim investigator. I'd missed that aspect of our relationship lately. Maybe now was the time to give it another try.

"So," Peggy said, "Are you going to ask him to join you or not?"

"Let me think about it," I replied. "He may not even be able to get away, you know. Being a small-town lawyer could be keeping him busy."

"Or not. There's only one way to determine that," Peggy said. "And don't take too long thinking about it. In the meantime, let's take care of the rest of your travel arrangements. You'll need a rental car. Any special requests?"

"A Mustang, please. Definitely a convertible. White if possible."

"I'll do my best. Any thoughts on a motel?"

"I imagine the motel in Hog Jaw will be closed during the investigation. See if you can find me someplace close, though. And hopefully with a decent place to eat."

"Double bed? Room for two?" she asked.

I scowled and didn't respond.

Peggy tapped away on her key board. "Let's look at nearby towns." She pulled up a map on her computer then turned her monitor so we could both see it.

Tiffany Allendale, the third member of our investigative team, chose that moment to pop in to check on our current caseload. She was slightly overdressed as usual, in a pale gray business suit, frilly white blouse, skirt just above the knee and low heels. The concept of business casual was still a challenge for her.

"Good morning, folks," she chirped. "Isn't it a simply gorgeous day?" Tiffany tended to be excessively cheerful. Not a bad trait - most of the time. "What's new in the wonderful world of insurance disasters?" she asked.

"Have a seat, Tiff," I said. I gave her a brief overview of our new case.

She furrowed her brow for a few moments, then said, "Sounds like fun to me. I mean, really, how could you not love a trip to a place called Hog Jaw?" She leaned over to get a closer look at the map on Peggy's monitor. "Wow. Looks like Hog Jaw Tennessee is way out in the back of beyond."

"The back of beyond?" Peggy asked. "What does that even mean?"

"It's the polite way of saying the ass end of nowhere," Tiffany replied.

I couldn't have said it better myself.

Peggy shrugged. "You mean it's rural."

"Right." Tiffany continued to peer at the map on Peggy's screen. "Oh my goodness, Amy! Did you see where Hog Jaw is located?"

"All I know so far is that it's in western Tennessee," I said.

Tiffany grinned from ear to ear. "It is. And it's also not far from the Pinson Mounds."

The amateur archaeologist in me jumped for joy. "Pinson? Wow! I've been wanting to visit those mounds for ages." Tiffany and I had both studied archaeology in college. It was one of the many things we had in common.

"The Pinson Mounds?" Peggy asked. "What in the name of heaven are they? And why are we so thrilled about them?"

Being the boss, it was my privilege to educate her. "They're ancient ceremonial and burial mounds built by an early civilization in North America—not unlike the pyramids in Egypt, but constructed of earth rather than stone. They were built somewhere around 1,000 BC. Their location was fairly central to indigenous people from all over North America. This made Pinson the perfect place for the tribes to gather for their summer meetings, sort of like pow-wows."

Tiffany jumped in. "All sorts of rituals were performed there. Word is that the entire area around Pinson is somewhat magical."

"Magical? *And* prehistoric?" Peggy shook her head. "You know, you two really are a couple of hopeless nerds."

"Well, heaven knows we could all use a little magic in our lives," I said, then added, "Pinson will make a nice side trip for me—when my work is done, of course." I may have been stretching the truth a little there, but so what? Peggy and Tiffany wouldn't tattle on me.

"Whatever floats your proverbial boat," Peggy said. "I hope you have a wonderful time there. Can't wait to hear all about it." Her tone of voice wasn't lost on me. Understatement bordering on sarcasm was one of her finer skills.

"In the meantime, Ladies," I said, "let's get back to business. We're looking at a potentially complicated claim in a part of the country unfamiliar to me. I can use all the help I can get to sort it all out."

"Sure thing, Boss," Peggy said. "Just tell us what you need."

I gave that a moment of thought. "Just do your usual great job of keeping the department on the straight and narrow while I'm gone. You're good at that, Peggy. Please keep an eye on things in general. And no matter what happens, don't let George interfere. If anything comes up that's above your pay grade, go directly to Mark."

George was my official office nemesis. He did what he could to ruin my day every chance he got. Peggy was good at keeping him at bay.

She gave me a brief salute. "No problem there."

"Most importantly, I'm going to need both of you to put your fabulous research skills to work and get me background information. You can split that up."

"Specifics?" Tiffany asked.

"Mark told me the incident was mentioned in the news media over the weekend. I'm thinking it must have been a slow news day. That might be a good place to start."

Tiffany made a note. "That means there should be information on YouTube and the online news services. I'll check the print media as well, both national and local to … what's the name of this place again?"

"Hog Jaw," I said.

"Yeah, right. How could I forget a name like that? I'm guessing you'll want the low-down on the citizens as well."

"Absolutely. Both the citizens of Hog Jaw and the local law enforcement folks."

"The official website for Tennessee should be good for that," Peggy suggested. "Not to mention Facebook and other social media. If anybody connected to this case has a Facebook page, I'll find it. Let's hope it turns out to be something noteworthy, or at least relevant."

I wished I had thought of that myself. I was making progress with my case of technophobia, but was no match for either Peggy or Tiffany. "Great. I know I can count on you ladies to do your usual thorough job. I'm going to head out now to get ready to leave first thing in the morning."

"I'll stop by on my way home to pick up Sam," Peggy said. "And if you need anything else in the meantime, just let me know." The look she gave me said "Like perhaps a ticket for Pete?"

"I told you I'll think about it."

Chapter 4

Tennessee

Tuesday

I agonized over the Pete question for the rest of the day. That evening, after a long and somewhat uncomfortable phone conversation, he decided to join me on the trip. If it didn't work, it didn't work, but we were willing to give it a try. He made his own travel arrangements and was able to get the same flight as me, but seated far away. That was probably for the best. It gave me quiet time to review the file Mark had given me and get my head ready for whatever awaited me in rural Tennessee.

We landed in Nashville shortly after noon. I telephoned Peggy from the airport as soon as we retrieved our luggage. I knew that I could text or email her, but I preferred the human touch. It's so much friendlier and leaves a lot less room for misunderstandings—in my humble opinion.

My first question for her was: "How's Sam?"

"He's doing fine, though I can tell he misses you already."

I wasn't worried about him missing me. Sam loved Peggy almost as much as he did me. Staying with her was like going on canine vacation for him.

"I've got you all fixed up," Peggy continued. "There's a Mustang convertible—color unknown -waiting for you at Savemore Auto Rental at the airport. You were right about the motel in Hog Jaw. It's closed until the investigation is completed. You're booked into the Snuggle Inn in Davisville. It's the closest place I could find to Hog Jaw. I hope it's OK and that it lives up to its name."

I ignored that remark. "Anything else?"

"I spoke with the local sheriff's office. They won't be able to meet with you until sometime tomorrow. I'll send you the contact details. And Lillie Taylor, the widow of the recently-deceased Jake, will be available tomorrow after she meets with the funeral director. I'll send you her info as well."

Peggy was nothing if not efficient.

"Thanks. Is there anything happening back in Cambridge that I should know about?"

Peggy laughed. "Only that George is gloating over the fact that you got sent to rural Tennessee. He said he hopes you have a wonderful time in the back woods. And he walks around humming that song from Deliverance."

"Whatever," was all I could say to that. *Let him gloat all he wants. It doesn't change the fact that I got promoted over him ages ago. And he now reports to me.* "Thanks for holding down the fort while I'm in the back woods, Peg. I'll be in touch."

We headed off to claim our rental car. The Mustang wasn't white, but a bright, shiny red. It was a convertible, and spotlessly clean. No complaints.

Before leaving the airport, Pete and I consulted the map the rental company gave us—so much more user-friendly than a GPS, at least for me. We located both Hog Jaw and the Snuggle Inn. Hog Jaw was immediately off the interstate. But that would be a boring ride and it was a beautiful spring day. Since I wouldn't be able to accomplish much that afternoon anyway, we decided to take the back roads, through small towns, back woods and farmland. We put the top down and settled in for what we expected to be a pleasant, peaceful drive in rural Tennessee.

Actually getting out of the airport, around Nashville and onto Route 70 west, wasn't at all peaceful or pleasant, but we managed to maneuver our way through it without incident. Once we were away from the city, the air became fresh and clean and smelling subtly of rosemary and sage. We passed through several tiny towns on Route 70, all neat and quiet, and rather reminiscent of what America must have been like in the 1950s. Quite a change from the hustle and bustle of Cambridge or Boston. Interesting enough, but I didn't think I'd want to live there.

We stopped for lunch at a Sonic in a town called Madrid. We couldn't help ourselves. The aroma of salty hot grease called to us from two blocks away, rather like an olfactory magnet. We were hungry. Breakfast had been early, and I never liked to miss a meal if I could avoid it. Besides, I'd never been to a Sonic before. And I was always in the mood for a cheeseburger and onion rings.

An hour or so after lunch, we picked up a secondary road heading south. And total peace and quiet took over in a heartbeat. The only sounds we heard were the wind passing through the trees and the birds having a mid-day chat. The road was narrow and winding. We reduced our speed and drove for what seemed like forever without spotting another car, nothing but fields at first, eventually followed by forests with no end in sight. Pretty nice.

"I read up on your case on the plane," Pete told me. "There were several news articles online. It could prove to be interesting. Having two guns and two bodies sounds to me like the ending of a gunfight back in the old west."

I gave that some thought. "If that's actually what happened."

"What do you think happened?" he asked. "Do you think the wife did it?" he asked.

"No way."

He turned and gave me a curious look. "Why not? Wouldn't the widow be the usual suspect in a life insurance case?"

"Maybe if the policy had been in effect for a long time," I told him. "This one was barely six months old. I have a difficult time believing any woman would be stupid enough to kill her husband that early in the policy term and expect to get away with it."

"I see what you mean," he said.

"Not only that," I added, "but guns are not usually a woman's weapon of choice when it comes to murder. Women are more inclined to use poison, or to create some sort of alleged accident."

"And you know this how?" he asked.

"It's my job."

"I'll take your word for that," Pete said. "And let's not forget that there was a second victim here. That trucker. How does he fit in? What exactly are we looking at? Double murder? Murder suicide? Perhaps something even more sinister?"

I loved the fact that he said we. Perhaps there was hope for us. "The jury is out on everything until we see the forensic reports," I told him.

"Right," he said. "They should help us figure out who shot whom first, though perhaps not why."

"And the why, my friend, is what we're here to learn. The outcome could be worth $500,000 to NEC&I."

I sat back in the passenger seat to breathe in the sweet country air and enjoy the view. Then I noticed something curious along the side of the road. "Pete, take a look at this."

"What's that?" He slowed down.

"Here, on the right. About ten or twelve feet in from the road," I pointed. "There's a chain link fence. A big, heavy chain link fence with barbed wire on the top. I first noticed it a few minutes ago. It seems a bit odd out here in farm country. It makes me wonder what somebody might be trying to keep in—or out."

Pete made his thoughtful lawyer face. "You're right. It is somehow out of place."

We watched the chain link fence in the forest for another mile or so. Then there was a break in it—a paved driveway leading up a small hill to a large building complex. A metal barrier sat a few feet up the hill, discouraging unwanted visitors. A small sign at the barred entry read: Armstrong Industries. No indication as to what these industries might be. Curious.

We drove on.

It was nearly 5:00 when we located the Snuggle Inn on the outskirts of a town named Davisville, a few miles outside of Hog Jaw. It was a small motel, nothing fancy, but looked clean and newly-renovated. Its major selling points appeared to be AC and free TV. Pete waited in the car while I went to sign in. The desk clerk was a friendly young woman, dressed in tight blue jeans and a Tennessee Titans tee shirt. She spoke with a thick southern drawl. "Welcome to Tennessee," she greeted me. "Amy Lynch, room for two, right?"

I forced a smile and nodded.

"Your room's all set, Ms. Lynch, one double bed and a pull-out couch. Coffee machine here is out of order, so you'll need to go to the diner across the street in the morning," she told me, handing me the key. "I hope that's not a problem."

I would have preferred separate beds, either singles or doubles, just to make our "reunion" a bit less awkward. I should have mentioned this to Peggy. Oh well, I couldn't find fault with her intentions.

Once in the room, Pete dumped his suitcase and laptop on the couch. He called his office to make sure everything was fine there. By the time he got off the phone, it was 6:30 and I was starved. We had a quick dinner at the local diner—southern fried chicken and more mashed potatoes than either of us needed. I passed on the boiled okra.

Back in the motel, I got to feeling a bit awkward. This was the first time Pete and I had shared a room since the unpleasant incident in San Luis Obispo. Neither of us mentioned that fact. We watched a bit of mindless TV and tried to relax, carefully avoiding any heavy relationship conversation. Still, it was nice to have some low-key, quiet Amy and Pete time—even if we didn't exactly snuggle. We needed this time together if we were ever going to repair our relationship. One small step at a time. We both wanted it to work.

I fell asleep during the late news. A while later, Pete roused me from my sleep. "Wake up, Ames. You've got to see this."

I yawned. "What?"

"Here." He pointed to his laptop screen. "I did some research on Armstrong Industries, that place we passed this afternoon."

"And? Did you find anything interesting?"

"You wouldn't believe what they do."

"So tell me," I said. "What?"

Pete turned to me with a dead serious look on his face. "They manufacture bombs. Their largest customer is the U.S. Department of Defense. What do you think about that?"

I thought about it for a moment, then said, "I think it makes perfect sense. Somebody's got to manufacture explosives somewhere. Better to do so on a remote back-country road. Less chance of problems—or injury to the public."

"That's for sure," he agreed.

Now I was fully awake. "What else did you research while I was sleeping?"

"Those ceremonial mounds that you told me about," he said. "At Pinson. You're right. They sound fascinating. Definitely worth a side trip. As is Beale Street in Memphis. It seems there's a lot more to see and do in rural Tennessee than I expected."

I nodded and frowned at the same time. "No argument there, my friend. There's just one minor problem."

"And what's that?"

"Time. Mark wants this case wrapped up quickly. We may not have much time for fun." I hoped I was wrong about that.

Chapter 5

Wednesday morning

I was awake early the next morning after a fitful sleep filled with dreams of bombs dropping on Beale Street while indigenous peoples danced around. Interesting, but not particularly restful.

Pete and I returned to the local diner where we feasted on a "cholesterol special" breakfast—eggs, sausages and too many home fries—then headed out for Hog Jaw, Tennessee. I had a 9:30 meeting with the local sheriff and wanted a chance to check the town out first.

Mark's description of Hog Jaw proved to be right on the money. It was barely more than a truck stop just off the interstate. It sat at the foot of the aptly named Hog Jaw Mountain. There were thick woods nearby, and signs indicating hiking paths. The town itself consisted of a motel, a diner and a gas station/convenience store. A sign said "Welcome to Hog Jaw / Population 37." Nary a soul nor a vehicle anywhere in sight. No houses either. Jake Taylor was dead. I wondered where the other 36 residents actually lived.

The motel was the type you would have seen on Route 66 in the 1950s: eight guest rooms, each with parking directly outside the door; an office between rooms 2 and 3. A sign in the office window said "Closed."

There was yellow police tape across the door to room 8, aka the scene of the crime.

The sign in the window of the Hog Jaw Diner boasted: "The best cornbread in West Tennessee". We would have to see about that. The gas station had a huge parking area off to the side, probably to accommodate trucks coming in off the highway. It offered expert and speedy tune-ups and oil changes. I hoped we wouldn't need either. Both businesses were closed at the moment, as was the small convenience store between the diner and the gas station.

We parked in the motel lot and sat in the car listening to the local country music station until the sheriff's vehicle pulled up—nearly half an hour late. Perhaps he was functioning on country time. Pete wanted to go exploring while I did my thing with the local law enforcement. I kissed him good-bye and made him promise to stay safe and keep in touch, then turned my attention to the sheriff.

He was a tall man, well over six feet. He had a wiry build, a five o'clock shadow and a gentle smile. He appeared to be in his late thirties or early forties and somewhat overtired. "Ms. Lynch?" he said. "I'm Emmet Snow. Sorry about the wait. Good to meet you."

"Likewise." I shook his outstretched hand.

"I sure hope you're okay chatting out here in the parking lot," he said. "It's not ideal, but there aren't any other options. And we do have some privacy here at the moment."

"It's fine."

"We sure appreciate you coming all the way from Boston to work with us on this case," he continued. "I know you're not actually law enforcement, but an investigator is an investigator and another set of eyes with a different point of view never hurts."

One could only hope that was so.

"I'm happy to do my part," I told him. "New England Casualty and Indemnity is as interested in getting to the bottom of this case as you are."

Sheriff Snow frowned. "I have to admit that this type of situation is new to me. We don't get a lot of murders around here, you know."

It occurred to me that perhaps that had something to do with the size of the population.

I pulled out my phone and asked, "Do you mind if I record this?"

"Not a problem." He gave me what looked like a genuine smile and picked up where he had left off. "As a matter of fact, I've been the sheriff in these parts for nearly fifteen years now and this is my first murder. Crime in rural Tennessee is usually limited to bar fights and domestic abuse. And let me tell you, that can get a bit tricky, seeing as how everybody knows everybody else around here. And a lot of them are related."

I hadn't thought about that. "Am I correct in assuming that you knew the victims?"

"Not the trucker. Just Jake, I've known him for years. He was a few years behind me in school, but in a small town like this, like I said, everybody knew everybody." A sad smile passed across his face. "I grew up with Jake's wife Lillie as well. We were best friends all through school. She was the first girl I ever kissed. And, you know, you never get over your first love."

Sheriff Snow was right about that. I choked back a memory or two and waited to see what he'd say next.

He let out a little laugh. "Yep, Lillie may not have been the brightest girl in the class, but she sure was cute. And quite the little flirt, let me tell you. All the guys wanted to date her, but she chose me. That is, at least until Jake caught her attention."

Hmmm. And how did Sheriff Snow feel about that? Did that give him a motive to kill Jake? I filed that thought away in my brain for the moment and returned to my task at hand. "Can you walk me through what happened the other night?"

"Sure thing." He closed his eyes as if to focus his memory. "The call came in a little after 11:00, on the local 911 line. Woke me up. But keep that to yourself, please. I don't usually do the overnight shift so I'm not used to being awake at that hour. Normally I do mornings and early afternoons. Overnight is Micah's job. But his wife went into labor that afternoon, so I had no choice. Didn't even get a chance to have supper before going in to relieve him."

Hmmm. So perhaps Sheriff Snow wasn't exactly at his best?

"Who was it that called?"

"One of the other motel guests. A local guy named Chuck. He heard Lillie's screams and went to see what was happening. From what he told me, Lillie was outside of room 8, shouting and shaking and crying something awful about somebody being hurt. I've got to give Chuck credit for being level-headed. He had the good sense not to go into the room, just stayed outside on the walkway, doing his best to calm Lillie down until I arrived."

"Please tell me you have Chuck's full name and contact information."

"I sure do. It's a good thing that he's a local fellow. He can be available for questioning any time."

That was a lucky break, though I couldn't help but wonder what a local resident was doing at the local motel in the middle of the night in the middle of the week. "What did you do after the call came in?" I asked.

"The first thing was to contact the local first responders. I needed to get an ambulance out there as fast as possible—in case somebody was still alive. Chuck's call had been unclear about that. Then I called Detective Mike Olin at the Highway Patrol office in Jackson. That's where the closest coroner and forensic team are located. After that, I high-tailed it over to Hog Jaw to secure the scene and see what I could do for Lillie."

"How long did it take you to get there?"

"Maybe twenty minutes," he said. "No traffic at that time of night. And I had the lights and the siren going."

"What did you find when you arrived?" I asked.

"Lillie and Chuck were sitting on the pavement outside room 8. He was doing his best to keep her calm. It wasn't working so well. The poor thing was beyond upset, crying so hard I could barely understand what she was telling me. All I got out of her was that somebody had been shot in room 8 and there was blood everywhere."

"Is that what you saw when you went into the room?" I prompted.

"Didn't go in right away," he told me.

"Why not?" *Wasn't that your job?*

"The ambulance showed up then, with the Highway Patrol car right behind it. I decided to let those folks do their thing first. Taking care of Lillie was more important to me at that point. I told Chuck to stick around. A couple other motel guests were out and about by then, curious to see what was going on. I wanted to make sure they didn't disappear before I got a chance to interview them, or at least get their contact info. I telephoned my deputy to come by to help me with that."

Sounded to me like a sensible enough plan, except for one thing. "Didn't you say your deputy was busy with his wife giving birth?"

Snow let out a small chuckle. "That was Micah. Other deputy's name is Lucas. He usually works the afternoon shift. Thank the lord he was able to come over and help me out."

"Hog Jaw has two deputies?" I asked.

"We serve the whole county," he told me.

That made sense.

"How many other motel guests were there?" I asked.

"Four other rooms were occupied. Two bikers. One trucker. And Chuck. I've got their statements and their contact information for you here." He handed me a fat manila envelope.

That was good work. I hoped it would make interesting reading.

Snow continued his narrative. "I also called Lillie's sister Noreen. She lives pretty close by and has a good practical head on her shoulders. Lillie needed a place to stay for a while. And I didn't want her to be alone."

"What's Noreen's last name?" I asked.

"It's Evans. Her address and phone number are in that envelope with the statements."

"That was good thinking. Thanks."

He nodded. "Right. I had to do something to help Lillie. I woke Noreen up out of a dead sleep. She showed up not long after the State Police and the coroner arrived. She took Lillie home with her."

"Did the State Police take Lillie's statement first?"

Sheriff Snow shook his head. "Nope, not right then. I managed to convince Officer Olin to let her leave with her sister and interview her the next day, you know, once she'd had a chance to calm down."

That was a deviation from standard procedure. Probably not the best idea, but I did understand the sheriff's motivation. "Is Lillie still at her sister's?"

"As far as I know. She must be, since the motel's still closed. Lillie lives here, you know, in the apartment off the motel office."

"Did you contact anybody else at that time? Lillie or Jake's family members perhaps? To let them know what happened?"

"Nope," he said. "I figured it was best to let the crime scene folks do their job and I could deal with the rest later."

I guessed that made sense, in a lackadaisical sort of way. "What happened next?"

"Once Lillie was being seen to and Lucas had arrived, I joined the state team in the motel room." The look on his face suggested he wasn't thrilled to do so.

"Can you describe what you saw?"

Snow closed his eyes and frowned. "I'll never forget it. Poor Jake was on his back on the floor with blood all around his head and face. Lou Bancroft, the trucker, was on the floor across the room, leaning against the wall. There were blood stains on the wall and on the rug around him. And both men had guns in their hands."

"Do you think the two men shot each other?"

"Maybe. Or it could have been a murder-suicide. Depends on the timing. I'm waiting on the forensic report to figure that out. Hoping that'll tell us who shot first."

With two deaths so close together in time, I wasn't so sure that would work. There was not much point in mentioning that to Sheriff Snow right now though. Better to wait until all the facts were in.

Snow stared at the ground and spoke softly, as if talking to himself. "I don't know what difference the timing would make anyway. The fact is, both men are dead. And we have no idea why."

And the settlement of Jake's life insurance policy just might depend on that fact.

"Did you do a routine forensic check on the room?" I asked. "Personal items, fingerprints, that sort of thing?"

Snow shook his head. "Nope. I left that up to the state forensics team. They're the experts on that sort of thing."

It was looking to me like Sheriff Snow had left of lot of things for the state team to handle. "Where will your investigation go from here?" I asked.

"Nowhere."

"I beg your pardon?"

The sheriff stared at his feet. "My job is done here. The rest is up to Mike Olin and his crew. I'll be nearby if anybody needs me, but I'm pretty sure they can handle whatever needs doing." He looked at his watch. "Is there anything else I can do for you at the moment?"

"I have to see the room," I told him.

"Yeah. Right. You real sure you want to?" He furrowed his brow. "You know, it hasn't been cleaned yet. I mean, the bodies have been removed, but that's about it."

"I'll need photos of the scene in order to process the claim. Bureaucracy at its finest. Nothing happens until the paperwork is submitted."

That was stretching the truth, but I suspected Snow wouldn't realize that. Crime scenes were often full of surprises. And my natural nosiness had paid off more than once in the past. "It will only take a few minutes."

"Okay then. Let's go," he said as he reached into his pocket for the key.

Room 8 was a typical older, low-budget motel room. The furniture was old and sturdy looking, the carpet faded and threadbare in a few spots. Pretty much what you would have seen almost anywhere fifty or so years ago, except for the blood stains on the rug and the wall, and a few bullet holes in the wall and the furniture. The sad fact was that I had seen far worse—as far as both motel rooms and crime scenes go. I did a quick inspection, took lots of pictures. I would blow these up on my laptop later to search for clues as to what had actually happened in the room. Hope usually does spring eternal.

Chapter 6

Wednesday, Late morning

I had learned all I could from Sheriff Snow for the moment, and he was obviously eager to be on his way. With his deputy on paternity leave, the office was understaffed. He did, however, promise to contact me when he received the forensic reports or if anything else of interest came up. I thanked him for his time and texted Pete that I was done for the moment.

Pete arrived to pick me up within just a few minutes.

"Wow," I said to him as I jumped into the Mustang. "That was fast. Were you lurking just around the corner waiting for my call?"

He laughed. "Not exactly, but I was nearby."

"How about we put the top down?" I suggested. "It's a perfect day for it now that it has warmed up a bit."

"Good idea."

I sat back in the passenger seat to collect my thoughts and make a few notes while Pete dealt with the car.

"How did things go with the sheriff?" he asked.

"About as expected."

"Did you learn anything interesting?"

Good question. "I'm not sure yet," I told him. "So far everything seemed pretty routine. Sheriff Snow was the first law officer on the scene the night of the shooting. He did a decent enough job with the necessary preliminaries, although he didn't exactly strain himself. He had the good sense to realize the incident was beyond his experience and to call in the state police detectives and their forensic experts. I'm hoping to speak with them tomorrow. And with any luck, perhaps by then they will have determined who fired the first shot. That's looking like the critical question at the moment."

Ever the lawyer, Pete asked, "Were there any witnesses the night of the shooting?"

"Not to the incident itself, but there were a few motel guests. Sheriff Snow interviewed them and provided me with his notes as well as their contact information. I'll get in touch with all of them for interviews, hopefully tomorrow. You never know. Perhaps at least one of them may have seen or heard something helpful that night. Sometimes they don't even realize what may be important. I'll also have Peggy and Tiffany see what they can find out about them. Just to rule them out."

"Really?"

"It's better to leave no potential stone unturned," I told him. "And you never know, there's always a chance one of them may have been involved."

"That last bit may be wishful thinking on your part. Nevertheless, it sounds like you're moving in the right direction," Pete said. "What else is on the agenda for today?"

"I'm meeting with Lillie Taylor, the widow, at 2:00. I'm hoping you'll join me. It may be helpful to get a lawyer's point of view."

"Sure. I'd like that." He checked his watch. "It's a little after 11:00 now. Too early for lunch. How about we go for a tour of West Tennessee?"

It was a beautiful mild spring morning. A ride in the country sounded nice, particularly in a Mustang convertible. And I could use the time to clear my mind and sort out the case in my head. "Any place in particular you'd like to go?"

"Back to where I was earlier," he said, putting the car in gear. "To pick up where I left off when I got your text. And try to figure out exactly what it is that I saw."

My curiosity was sufficiently piqued. "Okay. I'll bite. Where were you? What were you doing there? And what did you see?"

Pete laughed. "Whoa, Ames. Let's take this one thing at a time. I started out just snooping around a little. Exploring the area. After all, this may be my one and only time in Hog Jaw, Tennessee. I wanted to make sure I didn't miss anything. I decided my sense of adventure could use a boost. Life has been quiet lately."

It was about time my poor prosaic Pete realized that. I chose not to point that out to him. Maybe later. "I'm guessing you found something of interest."

He frowned. "I'm not sure. Something a bit odd, at any rate."

"Explain, please."

"How about I show you instead?" he suggested. He put the Mustang in gear and headed away from beautiful downtown Hog Jaw.

"Works for me." I fastened my seat belt. "Let's go."

When we were outside of town, Pete said, "If I remember my high school history correctly, I believe there used to be moonshiners in the hills of rural Tennessee. Do you think there might be any of them left?"

Before I could respond to that, Pete slowed down and pointed to the right. "Here we are."

I looked around and saw nothing but trees. "Here we are where?"

"Hog Jaw Road," he said. "See the sign?"

I directed my gaze to where he was pointing. "I see the sign. Having trouble believing it though. This can't really be a road."

He rolled his eyes. "I know what you mean, but my GPS would disagree with you."

"Your GPS might be mistaken," I said. "Really. Take a look. There's a dirt path—no pavement at all from what I can see. It winds up a steep hill and into a forest. The alleged road is barely wide enough for one average sized vehicle. There's a lovely creek down on the left, nice to look at, but we can do that from here and not risk falling in. So tell me, my friend, exactly what about this picture says road to you?"

"Everything you're saying is true," he said. "Nevertheless, this is a road. And you're about to discover why I found it interesting."

"Does this mean you actually intend to drive up that hill?" I shuddered at the thought.

"I do indeed. And, by the way, the locals call it a mountain, not a hill."

"And what will happen when - or should I say if? - we encounter another vehicle coming in the opposite direction? Sounds like the makings of a head-on crash to me. Either that or somebody would end up off the road, maybe into the creek on the left. And let's not even talk about another car trying to pass us."

Pete flashed me a lovely smile. "We'll be fine, Ames. Just trust me."

I heaved a sigh. "Okay. But this better be good. Will it explain why you were asking about moonshiners?"

"Perhaps. After all, just look at this. A dirt road up a hill, excuse me, up a mountain, in the woods in the country. An exceptionally well-maintained dirt road. A wonderful place for an illegal still, don't you think?"

He turned right and began driving up the mountain. It was steeper than I expected. I cringed as we arrived at a particularly tight right turn. "Slow down there, Pete." I gasped. "What if a car is coming at us heading down the hill right toward us?"

"We would have heard it by now."

I wasn't sure I believed that, but let it slide. "Or what if there's a deer, or other wildlife, in the road ahead?"

He slowed the car, but continued climbing up the hill. "We'll be fine, Ames. Just check out this road. It may be packed dirt, but there's not a rut or a rock anywhere. It's in excellent—actually better than excellent - condition. That made me curious to see what was up there. I couldn't help myself."

"Does that mean you've been up there already?"

"I have."

"And what did you discover?" I asked him.

Pete gave me a cryptic grin. "Absolutely nothing. That's what interests me the most. I mean, really, the road leads nowhere except to the other side of the mountain. There's nothing on it, yet it's in perfect shape."

I picked up on his thoughts. "So the question becomes who is maintaining this road to nowhere, and why."

He grinned. "I'm thinking possibly moonshiners? I decided it would be good to take a second look, and with a second pair of eyes."

It was hard to argue with his reasoning. "Okay. Let's go for it."

We continued up the mountain.

Hog Jaw Road was scenic, lined by trees in all their early spring glory. There was a small unpaved parking area with signs indicating the way to the hiking path. We also passed two tiny cemeteries along the way— each with two lonesome gravestones worn down by weather and time. We couldn't quite make out the names on them from the car. And I wasn't about to get out. Not with the steep drop on the left way down into a stream. One gravestone had toppled over. Other than that, Pete was right. There was nothing on the road. Absolutely nothing. In the end, Hog Jaw Road simply took us to the end of Hog Jaw Road.

Pete wasn't about to give up on it, though. "Next time, I'm thinking about coming up here on foot. In hiking boots."

"You brought hiking boots?" I asked. "Whatever for?"

"Because you never know. It's always good to be prepared. We passed a path on the right a little way back. Not wide enough for a car. I'd like to check that out on foot to see where it goes. I'm hoping you'll join me for that."

"Right now?" I glanced down at my casual business attire and wished I'd worn my sneakers.

He shook his head. "Perhaps tomorrow?"

I wasn't so sure about that. We'd have to see.

Chapter 7

Wednesday, Noonish

Once off Hog Jaw Road, we headed northwest toward Upton, where Lillie Taylor was staying with her sister. Having plenty of time to spare before my appointment, we stuck to back roads and tiny towns, driving past acres and acres of cotton fields. It was a pleasant ride—relaxing, and so very different from what I was used to in the Greater Boston area.

We pulled into a gas station in one small town looking to have a quick lunch. I had heard stories about Tennessee gas stations selling fried chicken and was eager to try it for myself. Surprisingly enough, it was pretty tasty.

We arrived at Lillie's sister Noreen's house at exactly 2:00. I loved it when we timed things just right. It was a small ranch-style house with an attached carport, sitting in the center of a good-sized luscious green lawn. A middle-aged woman dressed in neatly-pressed jeans, a tie-dyed tee shirt and well-worn sneakers met us at the door. She greeted us with smiling lips and a slightly furrowed brow. "Ms. Lynch?"

"Yes. And this is my assistant, Pete Devereaux." For some reason, I rather enjoyed referring to Pete as that.

"I'm Noreen Evans, Lillie's sister. Please, come this way." She swept her arm into the house to usher us through the doorway. "Lillie's sitting in the back yard. It's such a lovely day I thought it would be nice for us all to chat out there."

We followed Noreen through the house. It was neat and clean and vaguely reminiscent of the 1970s. It smelled like Lemon Pledge. "How is Lillie doing?" I asked.

Noreen stopped before we reached the back door. "She is so-so. The doctor prescribed her a mild sedative, just enough to keep her calm. She's been sleeping a lot, and not saying much of anything, but don't worry. She's awake and alert enough now. I'm sure she's fine to speak with you."

I gave Noreen what I hoped was my most sincere smile. "I'm sure this is all very difficult for both you and your sister."

"You've got that right," Noreen said. "Finding Jake dead was horrible enough, but now Lillie can't even lay the poor guy to rest. She discussed the arrangements with the funeral director, told him exactly what she wanted. The trouble is they can't set a date until the coroner's office releases the body. And they seem to be taking their own sweet time with that. On top of everything else, Lillie is absolutely distraught about the motel being closed, even for just a few days. She's worried about losing business. It's all taking a terrible toll on her."

Pete spoke up. "We'll do our best to make this as painless as possible for her."

His words came across as somewhat trite and empty, yet I was certain he meant them sincerely.

Noreen stiffened. "I hope so. Right now Lillie just needs to get all this unpleasant business over with as soon as possible. The sooner things are settled and she can get back to the motel, and get on with her life, the better off she'll be. Keeping busy is the best medicine, you know."

Having once been in a situation similar to Lillie's, I wasn't sure I agreed with that, but I held my tongue. No sense annoying a witness, at least not at the moment.

"Anyway, I'm glad we have a chance to speak before you see Lillie," Noreen added. "To make sure we're all on the same page. Do you have any idea how long it'll be before she gets the life insurance check?"

Nothing like getting directly to the point. "That depends on how things go with the sheriff and the forensics folks," I replied. "We can't settle the claim until their investigations are complete. And we have all the facts." Sometimes the truth hurts.

Noreen's mouth fell open. Wide-eyed, she asked, "What do you mean by that? Is there some kind of problem?"

"Probably not." I tried to sound reassuring, but wasn't quite sure I pulled it off. "The main issue is that, as of today, we still don't have an official cause of death. That's a show-stopper in the life insurance business."

"Being shot in the head doesn't do it?" Noreen's voice reeked of sarcasm.

"I'm afraid not. The question is who fired that shot?" I said. "The answer to that could tell us if it was murder or suicide."

"Good lord," Noreen said. "Are you telling me the policy won't pay if Jake killed himself? That doesn't sound right."

The best I could tell her was, "It's too soon to tell. When a policy is less than six months old, there is always some additional investigation to be done. It's all standard procedure." After a moment, I added, "Do you think there's any chance Jake did kill himself?"

"No way," she snapped. "The man was too much of a coward to do such a thing." After a moment, she added, "Please don't tell Lillie I said that."

"Not a problem," I told her. "Can we speak with Lillie now?"

Noreen frowned and opened the back door. We followed her out onto a small patio with a few lawn chairs in a semi-circle on the paved area. The yard beyond contained a good-sized vegetable garden.

Lillie looked up and gave us a forlorn little smile. She was petite and pale and tired looking, her hair dyed blonde, her eyes a dull blue. You're here about Jake's life insurance, right?" she asked.

"Yes. Please accept my condolences on the death of your husband." I said.

Lillie lowered her eyes and murmured, "Thanks."

"And thank you for taking the time to speak with us," I added. "I'll make this as quick and easy as I can. I need some information from you in order to process the claim."

She nodded. "What can I tell you?"

"I pulled out my phone. "Do you mind if I record this?"

Noreen appeared aghast at that idea, but had the good sense not to say anything.

Lillie shrugged. "No problem."

I began with the easy stuff. "How long have you and Jake been married?"

"Nearly twenty years. I was barely eighteen. Just out of high school."

Pete sat up straight. "That's a long time. Why did you wait until now to take out a life insurance policy on him?"

I loved having Pete there to address the difficult issues. We could do the insurance version of good cop / bad cop.

Lillie answered without a moment's hesitation, "Jake's brother Andy died suddenly about a year ago. Heart attack. He was far too young. It put the fear of God into Jake. We bought the life insurance not long after that. Seemed like the thing to do."

"Did you get a policy for yourself as well?" Pete continued.

Lillie shook her head. "Not yet."

Not a good answer. I waited, hoping she'd explain.

"We've been on a really tight budget lately," she said. "Had to do some repairs and updates on the motel. It was more expensive than we expected."

"I understand," I said, even though I wasn't sure I did.

"So will I be getting the insurance check soon?" she asked. "I hate to admit it, but I really need the money."

"I'm afraid it's going to take a little bit of time," I told her. "My boss insists that I dot all the I's and cross all the T's before we issue a check. I'll hurry it along as best I can."

Lillie frowned, but didn't say anything.

"Do you have any children?" I asked. That probably didn't matter, but it was good to be thorough.

"No. I'm sorry to say we don't."

I waited to see if she'd provide any details. She didn't. And based on the sad look in her eyes, I decided to drop that line of questioning, at least for the moment. "How long have you had the motel?"

"A little over twenty years. It was a wedding present from Jake's parents."

"I imagine it's a busy place," I continued. "Being located right off the interstate." I was lying about that, not quite able to imagine why anybody would exit the interstate to stay in a place named Hog Jaw. If they went a couple of hours to the east or the west, they could stay in someplace cool like Memphis or Nashville.

Lillie said, "It keeps us both busy enough. We get a lot of regular guests, mostly truckers who come by every week or so. And then there are the lost tourists. You know, folks who took a wrong turn off the interstate. We also get some locals, lovers who have no business being there. I do my best to turn a blind eye to that. After all, it's not my place to judge people. And their money is as good as anybody else's."

"Don't forget about the bikers," Noreen reminded her.

"Right. Yeah. Over the last year or two, we've had members of a motorcycle club staying with us off and on. They love their weekend rides on the back roads around here."

"Do they give you any trouble?" Pete asked.

Lillie shook her head. "Nope. They're all pretty nice guys."

I filed that idea away for the moment. "Please walk us through what happened on the night Jake died," I said to Lillie.

Her eyes darkened. A single sob escaped from her lips.

"It's all right, dear," Noreen said. "Just take it slow and easy."

"It was getting late," Lillie began. "Some time around eleven. Jake and I were in the motel office."

"Are you usually in the office that late?" I asked.

She shook her head. "No. We live in the apartment right off the office. That's normally where we'd be in the evening. And if anybody arrived looking for a room, we'd hear them just fine. But our television was on the fritz and there was a movie we wanted to see. So we were watching it on the set in the office."

That seemed reasonable enough. "And you got a call?" I prompted her.

She nodded. "Right. From the guest in room 8."

"What was his name?" I asked.

"Lou Bancroft. He's a regular. A trucker. Very nice guy. We usually see him at least four or five times a month."

"How well do you know him?"

Lillie frowned. "Well enough, I suppose. Like I said, he was a regular."

My next question was: "Why was he calling at that hour? Was there a problem?"

"He was concerned about a noise he had heard."

"Did he sound upset?" Pete asked.

Lillie frowned. "I couldn't say. I didn't speak with him. Jake answered the phone."

Pete continued, "Was Lou Bancroft the nervous type? The kind to be concerned about a noise in the night?"

"Not really," Lillie replied. "From what I knew of the guy, I was surprised he was even awake at that hour. Normally he wasn't a night owl. He was all about lights out early and up and out well before six o'clock in the morning."

"So what do you think was keeping him up that night?" I asked. "The noise that he heard?"

Lillie shrugged. "I guess so."

"What sort of noise was it?" Pete asked.

"Beats me. Like I said, I didn't speak with him. Jake said he'd go to Lou's room and check it out. And for some reason he decided to bring the gun. It was late. It was dark. He said he wanted it with him just in case..."

"Just in case what?" I asked.

"I wish I knew," was Lillie's reply. "Anyway, Jake went to the drawer where we keep the gun, locked away safe and sound. And it wasn't there."

Not a good surprise. "Did you look for it?" I asked.

"Sure did," she said. "We searched everywhere. Didn't find it though."

And yet there was a gun in Jakes's hand when he was found. That made no sense. So far, the assumption had been that the weapon was his. I chose not to address this discrepancy at the time. Better to wait and see where our conversation might go.

Pete spoke up, "Is the gun licensed?"

Noreen chose to respond to that. "Of course it is."

Pete acknowledged that fact then asked Lillie, "How long was Jake gone?"

"Nearly an hour. I got worried when I hadn't heard from him. I decided to go over to room 8 and see for myself what was going on."

As much as I hated to, I asked, "And what did you see?"

Lillie inhaled deeply, then said, "Nothing at first. The room was dark. I switched on the light then regretted it right away. Like I told Emmet, you know, Sheriff Snow, Jake was on the floor and Lou was slumped on the far wall, both obviously dead."

Lillie stopped and stared at her shaking hands.

I gave her a few moments to regain her composure. "I'm sorry you had to relive that for me. Just a few more questions."

"Okay."

"Were Jake and Lou friends? Or close in any way?"

"Not really," she said. "I mean, they knew each other, sure, but I was usually the one who dealt with the guests."

Duly noted. "Did Jake have any enemies? Anybody unhappy with him who might have wished him harm?"

"Not a chance." Lillie let out a sad little laugh. "Jake was everybody's good buddy. They all loved him."

I sat back and thought for a few moments. What else might I want to know? "You and Jake ran the motel together, right?"

"Right."

"Who else worked there? Anybody who had access to the rooms? A chambermaid perhaps?"

"Not a soul," Lillie said. "Jake and I did all the work ourselves. We really couldn't afford to pay anybody else."

"So you were the one who had cleaned room 8?"

She nodded.

"When had you last cleaned it?" I asked.

Lillie didn't need to think about that. "That afternoon. Lou called to say he was on his way and I wanted everything clean and ready for him when he arrived. Not that the room wasn't already clean, though. I never let things like that go. But it was stuffy. I opened the windows to give it a good airing out."

Hmmm. "Do you mind cleaning rooms? It sounds like a lot of work to me."

"I don't mind it a bit," she said. "It's important to keep our guests happy. I like for everything to be squeaky clean. Particularly since Covid. I always bleach everything - the phone, the TV remote, whatever. Better not to take any chances, you know."

Lillie's cell phone rang. She glanced at it, then asked, "Do you mind if I take this? It's Emmet Snow. He may have news."

"Go ahead," I told her.

I didn't even try to hide the fact that I was listening in as she spoke with the sheriff. Why bother?

Lillie's face lit up and her shoulders relaxed. "Thanks, Emmet," she said. "That means a lot to me." She rang off, looked up at me with a hint of a smile, "He says we can reopen the motel tomorrow. Everything but room 8. The state cops and the coroner will be there sometime within the next few days to get their gear out and take a few final pictures. What a relief. I was so worried we wouldn't be open for the weekend business. We really can't afford to lose that kind of money."

Noreen didn't look too pleased.

"That is good news," I said, but wasn't sure I meant it. There was a chance that the place being open could interfere with my investigation.

Lillie rose from her chair. "I guess I better get started packing now, so I can move back in first thing tomorrow. I'll be happy to be home and back in business."

That was all I needed from Lillie at the moment. We thanked her for her time and said good-bye to her and her sister.

I felt a twinge of trouble as we headed to the car. I was pretty sure there was something else I should have asked Lillie. Something important. And I was damned if I could remember what it was.

Chapter 8

Wednesday afternoon

A few miles up the road from Lillie's sister's house, my brain kicked in. I grabbed my phone out of my bag and punched in a number.

"Who are you calling?" Pete asked.

"Sheriff Snow."

"Whatever for?"

Snow's voice came on the line before I could respond to Pete. "Ms. Lynch, hello. What can I do for you today?"

"Is there any way you can delay your final visit to the scene of the crime at the Hog Jaw Motel for a day or two?"

"Hmm. I suppose so, if it's important. What's up?" he asked.

"I'd like to take another look at the room," I told him. "With you accompanying me, of course. So there's no question as to what I may find there."

"That shouldn't be a problem. Anything in particular you're looking for?"

"I think so," I told him. "I'm not quite sure yet what it is. But I'm sure there's something else to be found there. I'm hoping that being in the room will jog something in my mind."

"Okay, sure. Why not?" he said. "Another day or two won't matter much in the grand scheme of things. I've got a lot going on tomorrow, though. Would Friday work for you? I can give you a call later and let you know what time."

"That would be great. Thanks." I ended the call, pleased that the local authorities were so flexible. A bit surprised, but definitely pleased.

Pete shot me a questioning look as I ended the call, but didn't ask what was on my mind. That was one of the things I loved about the guy. He didn't push, just bided his time and waited for me to volunteer information.

"What did you think of Lillie?" I asked him.

He gave that some thought. After a few moments, he replied, "Well, she seems to have her emotions under control, surprisingly so."

"Agreed. I'm assuming that's due to whatever sedative the doctor gave her. For now, anyway." I picked up my phone again.

Pete asked, "Who are you calling now?"

"Peggy," I said. "We need to touch base at some point. Doing so while you drive is a good use of my time."

Pete smiled. "Are you suddenly becoming efficient?"

"I am. And I'll take that as a compliment."

"Good idea."

Peggy picked up on the fourth ring, just before the line went into voice mail. Highly atypical behavior for her. "Hello to you," she said sounding slightly out of breath and nothing like her usual cheerful self.

Had I caught her at a bad time? I decided it might be best to get right down to business. "I'm putting you on speaker so Pete can listen in. So, tell me, how are things?"

"Everything's fine," Peggy sighed. "It has just been hugely busy here this week."

"Anything I need to know about?"

"Not really. Mostly just the same old hassles. They're all hitting at once right now. Nothing I can't handle," she said. "The trick is to find the time to deal with them."

I detected a note of disgruntlement in her voice. "Isn't Tiffany able to help?" I asked.

"She's trying to. Whenever she can get away from George. But he is being a royal pain in her backside since you left. Loading Tiffany down with all sorts of menial work and checking up on her constantly. Believe it or not, he is actually timing her coffee breaks. Can you believe that?"

Pete chose that moment to join the conversation. "Please tell us he isn't timing her trips to the Ladies' Room as well."

That elicited a small laugh from Peggy. "Not yet," she said. "But I'll keep you posted. In the meantime, tell me, how are things going out there in the back of beyond?"

"Not as fast as I'd hoped," I admitted. "Things seem to move somewhat slowly in the boondocks."

"What can I do to help?"

"Well, as long as you ask," I said, "please concentrate your attention on all things Hog Jaw, barring any absolute emergencies or crises, needless to say. I need any and all information you can find." I knew that was a mixed message, but didn't worry much about it. Peggy was a champion at prioritizing problems.

Peggy chuckled. "Gotcha. I'm working on that even as we speak."

"So tell me, what have you learned so far?" I asked. "I'm in the car, so how about you give me the abbreviated version now then email me the details later?"

"Sure thing. Let's begin with the main characters. "Lillie and Jake Taylor are both local to Hog Jaw. Jake's family has been there for generations. He and Lillie have owned and operated the motel for nearly twenty years. Their backgrounds border on the tedious. Jake's parents, Walter and Minnie Taylor, run the Hog Jaw Café. They're pretty lackluster as well.

Jake's brother Ike and his wife run the Hog Jaw Garage and convenience store. Ike was in minor trouble as a kid, mostly fighting and underage drinking. That ended about ten years ago when he married the deputy sheriff's cousin Jody."

"The recently deceased Lou Bancroft is from Kansas," she continued. "His widow, Doreen and his four children live in Bonner Springs. He has been a long-distance trucker all his adult life. Apparently a good, honest family man. Nothing untoward about him. At least not that I can find."

She clicked away at her keyboard for a few moments, then told me, "The greater Hog Jaw area of Tennessee is fairly quiet crime-wise. No crime statistics on the few local residents. Emmet Snow has been sheriff for a long time. He appears to be as honest as the day is long. His deputy, Lucas Fowler has been with him forever. He's clean as a whistle too. Micah Young, the other deputy, is new on the job. So far nothing of interest on him." She paused for a moment to come up for air.

"Moving right along," she continued, "State Police Detective Mike Olin is a solid, experienced lawman. He has a spotless record. The coroner, Lou Walker, has been on the job for over thirty years. That is a bit odd, since the job is officially a two-year position. He has no privileges at any area hospital. No idea why."

Peggy fell silent and let out a long slow sigh. "And that's all I have so far."

"It's a good start," I said. "It always helps to know something about folks before interviewing them, even if there's nothing nefarious going on in their lives. Good job."

"Thanks."

"Are you up for more sleuthing?" I asked.

"Always. Snooping into other people's business is the most interesting part of my job. What do you need?"

I groped around in my purse and retrieved the notes I'd taken earlier. "See what you can find out about the other motel guests that night.

There's a local fellow named Chuck Andrews, a trucker named Dick Greene, and two bikers—Buster Dolan and Gary Miller." I gave her the contact information the Sheriff had provided. "I want to speak with all of them."

"Got it," she said. "What else?"

"Just one more thing. See what you can learn about Armstrong Industries. They're located not far from Hog Jaw. So far, the only thing I know about them is that they manufacture bombs."

Peggy gasped. "Please tell me you're kidding."

"I seldom kid about anything as serious as weaponry."

"It doesn't sound quite right to me," she said. "Is it even legal?"

Pete decided to join the conversation at this point. "It must be legal, Peggy. From what I saw on their website, their largest customer is the United States Department of Defense."

I could almost hear the wheels turning in Peggy's head.

Finally she said, "Are you saying they have other customers as well? Should I worry about the fact that someone else out there is buying bombs?"

Pete laughed. "Explosives are also used in construction, you know. And mining."

"If you say so, Pete. I'll check them out. Is there anything else?"

"Not that I can think of at the moment," I said.

"All right, then. I'll get back to you when I have something to report. In the meantime, have a wonderful time in Hog Jaw."

As the call ended, Pete turned and gave me a curious grin.

"What?" I asked.

"Oh, nothing," he said. "I just love listening to you and Peggy work together. The two of you make a really good team."

"We do. And, by the way, please keep your eyes on the road. These country by-ways are full of surprising twists and turns."

"Right." He returned his gaze to the road ahead. "You know, you and I make a pretty good team as well. I've always enjoyed the times when we worked together on a case."

No argument there. "True. And I particularly enjoyed the time or two when you came to my rescue and saved me from serious harm," I said.

"I've been missing that connection these last few months," he said. "I've been missing us."

My eyes teared up. "Me too," was all I could say. I had particularly been missing the days when a look in his eyes or a touch of his hand could make me tingle all the way down to my toes. I wasn't quite sure I wanted to verbalize that to him just yet, though. It made me sound needy. And that was never good.

Pete cleared his throat. "I'm hoping we'll be able to work together like that again—soon, and often. Do you think we have a chance?"

"A good chance," I said. "We're finding our way back, but we still have some major work to do to get there. I'm willing to do that if you are." *And we need to be sure we both want the same things out of life. I had been wondering about that lately. But that's a conversation for another day., Right now I had a job to do, a case to close, and that had to be my priority. Or so I told myself.*

"I look forward to it," he said.

It was time to change the subject. Whatever Pete and I ended up doing, I felt we should go slowly. I wasn't up for any big emotional upheaval at the moment. Too much too soon hadn't served me well in the past. I really wanted to get it right this time.

In the meantime, I had a case to solve. "Okay, then," I said, "now that that's settled, let's talk about where we might get a decent dinner in this god-forsaken back-woods. I'm thinking we could grab something on the early side. That would give me time to review my notes and make some plans and a few phone calls this evening."

"Any idea where you might want to eat?"

"Let's go back to Hog Jaw and see if the diner there is open."

He gave me a funny look. "Do you think we'll get a decent dinner there?"

"I think we're about to find out."

Chapter 9

Late Wednesday afternoon

We pulled into Hog Jaw a little after 5:00. The gas station was open, and busy. Two large semis were at the pumps, with one more waiting in the wings. Apparently it paid to be located right off the interstate. I would need to find another time to speak with Jake's brother Ike.

The "open" sign was lit in the window of the Hog Jaw Diner. There were lights on inside. A few cars out front. It seemed the Hog Jaw dinner trade began on the early side.

"Looks like a popular place," Pete said to me. "Or perhaps the only game in town. So, shall we give it a try?"

"Absolutely," I replied. "I understand they have the best cornbread in West Tennessee. We need to check that out. And Jake Taylor's parents own the place. If the dinner crowd is light tonight, this could be a good opportunity to get their take on Jake's death and convey our condolences."

A bell jingled to announce our arrival when we opened the door. A delightful aroma greeted us. My appetite perked right up despite the substantial lunch I'd had. I took a good long look around. The diner was small—perhaps six tables plus a counter with six well-used stools. It appeared to be right out of the 1950s. Two middle-aged men in jeans and work boots sat at a table in the corner. Both were on the beefy side, looking tough and tired. Neither one smiled. My guess was truckers, apparently weary ones. A young couple with two small and surprisingly well-behaved children occupied a table in the middle of the room. Another table held four forty-something men. They all wore khaki pants, practical footwear and identical blue shirts with some sort of logo on them. My first thought was perhaps members of the local bowling league.

"Howdy, folks." A seventy-something man with a mop of white hair, an obviously forced smile and a black band around his left arm headed our way. "I'm Walt Taylor. How are you doing today?"

Jake's father, I presumed. "Just fine, thanks," I said. "And you?"

"Hanging in there," he said. He looked around the semi-busy little diner. "How about something with a view?" He guided us to a table for four by the window.

A woman I guessed to be Jake's mother came out from the kitchen. She was short and round with tight gray curls, dark piercing eyes and a sad look on her face. She too wore a black armband.

"That's my wife Minnie," Walt said, gazing in her direction. "She's the cook."

Minnie nodded and gave us the once-over. "You folks looking for dinner?"

Pete flashed her his most charming smile, "We are. What's on the menu tonight?"

Pete's smile had no effect. "Chicken pie," she told us wearily. "Or meat loaf. Both home-made. Both hot out of the oven. You want burgers and hot dogs, go to McDonald's."

So there! "What about cornbread?" I asked. "I understand it's the best in the area."

Not even that brought even the hint of a smile to her face. I couldn't blame the woman. Her son had just died.

"Cornbread comes with everything," she told us.

"How about chicken pie and cornbread?" I said.

"Same for me," Pete added.

She nodded, turned and headed back into the kitchen.

"Can I get you something to drink?" Walt offered.

"Wine?" I asked.

"Red or white?"

"What kind of white?" I crossed my fingers that it would be something other than Chardonnay.

Walt opened a fridge behind the counter. "Looks like it's just Sauvignon Blanc tonight," he said. "Chardonnay delivery is later this week."

"Sauvignon Blanc sounds fine to me," I said. *Whew!*

"I'll have a beer," Pete said. "An IPA if you have it.".

"Coming right up." Walt headed toward the bar, returning quickly with our beverages. His hands shook slightly as he placed them on the table. "You folks just passing through?" he asked. "Don't recall seeing you around here before."

I reached into my purse and produced my business card. "I'm Amy Lynch from New England Casualty and Indemnity. This is my associate, Pete Devereaux. We're here to handle the insurance end of the recent tragedy. I'm guessing you're Jake's father."

Walt nodded silently and avoided eye contact.

I sucked in a breath, then added. "We are so very sorry about Jake. I'm sure it has been very difficult for you."

"What can you do? Just gotta keep on keeping on," Walt sighed.

My heart went out to him.

"Did I just hear something about insurance?" Minnie called out from the kitchen. "Hold on. I'll be right there." She waddled toward us carrying a basket of cornbread and some butter. "Chicken pie will be another few minutes."

"You have my condolences on the death of your son," I said to her. "This must be very difficult for you."

Minnie nodded solemnly. "Ain't that the truth? It still doesn't seem real. My poor Jake. Such a good boy. He deserved a whole lot better than he got." She wiped a single tear from her cheek, then continued, "So what's up with the insurance? Will we be getting a check sometime soon? Life goes on, you know. We need to deal to with the damage to the motel and get back to business as soon as possible. Can't afford to lose business, you know. Nobody'll be wanting to eat here if they don't already have a place to stay nearby."

"Hold on a minute there, Minnie," Walt said. "There isn't going to be any check for us. That money will go to Lillie."

"Don't you think I know that?" Minnie snapped. "I'm just asking in general, that's all. Lord knows Lillie will be needing the money if she's going to keep the motel going without Jake around to do the real work. And, like I just said, our business depends on hers." Minnie looked me in the eye waiting for an answer.

"We've got to look into a few things before issuing payment," I told her. "For documentation. Nothing to worry about. Just routine life insurance business."

Minnie frowned. "What's to look into? It's life insurance. My son is dead. Where's the money?"

I gave her what I hoped was a sympathetic look. "It's standard procedure when a policy is less than six months old."

Minnie scowled. "Doesn't sound right to me."

"Also," I added, "I'll need to have the final reports from the coroner and the sheriff so I can document the file."

"How soon will that be?" she asked. "And what can we do to hurry them along?"

Walt broke in. "Now, Minnie. These things take time. We all have to be patient for a bit. Life will be back to normal soon enough."

"Life will never be back to normal," Minnie snapped at him.

Pete spoke up, possibly heading off an all-out argument between the two of them. "The good news is that the sheriff has given Lillie the green light to open the motel tomorrow, except for room 8."

Walt almost smiled. "That'll be a big help. We'll help Lillie to get the room back in order as soon as possible. The carpet will need to be replaced, the walls painted. She'll need a new easy chair as well. And as for the life insurance, that'll just have to wait. Right now, we need to help these nice folks out in any way we can." He turned to me. "So, what can we do for you?"

Minnie glanced toward the kitchen. "We can start by getting your dinner on the table. Hold on. I'll be right back."

We sampled the cornbread while waiting for Minnie to return. It was to die for.

"You'll have to be patient with Minnie," Walt told us. "She's taking this really hard."

"Of course she is," I said. It seemed like a good time to try some small talk. I turned my head toward the table where the four men sat and asked Walt, "Is that the local bowling league?"

Walt laughed. "Hell no. Those are some of the guys from Armstrong. You can tell by their shirts. They have the Armstrong logo on them."

I took a good look at the shirts. The logo showed the torso of a well-muscled man with his arms crossed over his chest. I figured it must mean something to somebody.

"Are they wearing the official Armstrong uniform?" I asked.

Walt shrugged. "I suppose so."

"Do you get a lot of the Armstrong folks here?" Pete asked.

"Sure do," Walt said. "Usually those same four guys. They come for dinner at least two or three times a week. There are a few others as well."

"Where do the rest of the Armstrong employees eat?" I asked.

Walt lifted his hands, palms up, in a "who knows" gesture. "Beats me. Not many other diners around here. Maybe they have a cafeteria over there in one of their buildings. Maybe those folks eat at home, wherever that may be. Too bad, too. They don't know what they're missing not coming here."

I couldn't help but admire Walt's attitude. "How long have you lived in Hog Jaw?" I asked, in an effort to turn the conversation toward something, anything, which might help with my investigation.

"All my life. My father opened this place, motel, diner and filling station back in the 40s. There was nothing here but an old coach road back then. Business picked up big time when the Interstate opened in the 60s. Things got even busier when Armstrong opened up in the 80s. I've worked here since I was a kid. Only job I ever had. Took over completely when my dad died back in 1982. Minnie and I used to run the whole operation. We were younger then. Little by little, our sons took over some things. Ike handles the filling station. Jake runs the motel."

Minnie appeared back at our table with plates of chicken pie." You mean he did until this week," she said with a sob.

My heart cried for her. "A real family business," I said. "Is everything owned jointly?" I would need this information to settle the claim.

"We gave the filling station and the motel to Ike and Jake as wedding presents," Walt told us, then added, "Please, folks, don't stand on ceremony. You should eat your food while it's hot."

I dug into my chicken pie with gusto. And my taste buds rejoiced.

"Whose name is on the deed to the motel?" Pete asked between bites of his chicken pie.

"Both Jake's and Lillie's," Minnie said with a big harrumph. "Why do you ask? Is that going to complicate things?"

I shook my head. "I don't see why it would. And, by the way, this is delicious."

"Minnie's a wonderful cook," Walt beamed. "We're lucky to have her."

I continued my questioning. "Will Lillie continue to run the motel?"

"No reason why she wouldn't," Walt said. "She's really good with people. The guests just love her. That's a mighty big deal in the motel business. People like to feel welcomed."

"It takes more than being friendly to run a motel," Minnie chimed in. "Jake always took care of the serious end of things. Lillie was never inclined in that direction. She preferred the social part of the business."

"Is there somebody who can take part of the job over now?" Pete said.

"There's Lillie's sister Noreen. Or maybe Ike's wife Jody," Walt told us. "Both of them have a pretty good head for business."

"Jody would be good for that," Minnie said. "That'd keep the place in the family, if you know what I mean."

Apparently, Lillie's sister didn't qualify as family. I didn't pursue the point with Minnie. Just filed it away for future reference.

Walt stepped away for a moment, returned to refill our glasses and said, "I'm kind of hoping Noreen will move in with Lillie. I don't like the thought of Lillie being alone in the office apartment."

I decided to stay out of that discussion. "What can you tell us about the night Jake died?"

"Not a thing," Walt said. "We live a few miles down the road. Didn't hear anything that night. Just the usual rumbles from the interstate. Had no idea about anything until we arrived the next morning to open up the diner. One of those bikers came in for breakfast. He told us what had happened." Jake frowned. "A little while later Emmet Snow came by to break the news to us. Don't really know what took him so long."

I couldn't help but wonder the same thing myself. "Do you remember the biker's name?" I asked.

Walt shook his head. "Sorry. Those guys all look the same to me."

That hit home with me. All I could picture was overweight guys with long white pony tails and sunglasses no matter what the weather was.

Minnie looked like she was about to say something but was distracted by the jingle of the bell on the door as two men entered the diner. "Gotta go," she said. "Looks like we're about to get busy." She and Walt headed to greet their new customers.

As Pete and I finished our meal, he asked, "What's your plan for tomorrow?"

"The state police detective and the coroner in Jackson in the morning. After that, I'll try to connect with the people who were staying at the motel last week. I plan to call them all when we get back to our motel. With any luck, somebody there may have something of interest to share with us."

Chapter 10

Thursday morning

Pete and I checked out of the Snuggle Inn first thing Thursday morning. Now that the Hog Jaw Motel was reopening, staying there simply made sense. It could only help my investigation. We stopped in Hog Jaw before heading into Jackson. Nobody was in the motel office when we arrived there. I left a note on the door asking them to save a room for us.

Pete was unusually quiet as we drove to Jackson. He had said very little since we left the diner the night before, mostly just sat staring at his laptop while I took care of some business. I considered asking him what was up, but decided not to. Better to wait things out and see what developed. At least that's what I told myself. I hoped it was the truth.

We took the scenic back roads and arrived in Jackson an hour and a half later. Detective Mike Olin greeted us at the door to his office. He was a tall man with perfect posture, a weather-worn complexion and the beginning of a middle-age paunch. "Good morning," he said without a trace of a smile. The office room reeked of day-old Egg McMuffins and stale coffee. I wished he'd open a window.

"Please have a seat. I understand you want to discuss the recent deaths in Hog Jaw. I can give you about an hour. Things are unusually busy here this week."

We sat. I pulled out my phone. "Do you mind if I record our conversation?"

"I'd rather you didn't," he said with a scowl. No explanation. Just a scowl.

Oh well. I dug into my purse for a notebook and pen. I was tempted to leave my phone on "record" in my purse where he wouldn't see it, then thought better about it. No point risking the wrath of the local authorities. I poised my pen and got straight to the point. There was no sense wasting time on social niceties with this man. "How is your investigation coming?" I asked.

"Stalled at the moment," he said. "Maybe permanently."

Not what I wanted to hear. "How so?"

He opened a file folder on his desk and stared at it for what seemed like far too long. "We don't know much more at the moment than we did the night of the incident. There was a shooting, or two actually. Both men fired their guns. Both men died. Lou Bancroft was a regular guest at the Hog Jaw Motel so he and Jake were acquainted. There's nothing so far to indicate any animosity or issues between them. It seems that most of Lou's interactions at the motel were with Lillie Taylor."

I stopped him right there. "Lillie told me that Jake couldn't find his gun before going over there."

"Well, looks like he must have found it," Olin shrugged. He paused for a moment, frowned, then continued, "We have Lillie's description of how things evolved that night, as well as some witness statements. I understand that Sheriff Snow has already given you copies of these, so there's no point in wasting time over them now. You can read them at your leisure. From what I know so far, nobody saw or heard anything."

"Did you interview the witnesses yourself?" Pete asked.

Olin shook his head. "There was no need to. Like I said we're busy here. And short-handed at the moment. I'm quite comfortable accepting Emmet Snow's information. The sheriff knows what he's doing."

I was considering questioning this lackadaisical procedure when the phone rang on Detective Olin's desk. He studied it for a few seconds, then ignored the call.

Within that short time, I decided to play nice and not antagonize Olin, at least not yet. "In your opinion, Detective Olin, how exactly did the shootings happen?' I asked.

"Good question. No real answer. Both men fired one or more shots. There were no bullets remaining in either weapon. Of course, we have no way of knowing how many bullets there were to begin with. The bottom line is that both men died. The situation could have been something right out of the O.K. Corral for all we know."

"That would suggest some sort of disagreement between them. Something serious enough that it led to violence," I said.

Olin shrugged. "I suppose so. The witness statements make no mention of an argument though. Odds are we may never know for sure. What can you do?"

Knowing for sure was a major factor in my investigation. I pushed on. "What about the timing? Were the shots simultaneous? Or is it more likely that one of them shot first? And the other returned his fire?"

Another shrug. "I can't see what possible difference that would make. The results are the same either way. Both men are dead."

The same results for him, perhaps, but not for me. And definitely not what I wanted, or needed, to hear. I couldn't pay or deny a claim based on an inconclusive cause of death on a death certificate.

"So where does that leave us?" I asked.

Olin scowled. "Pretty much nowhere, I'm sorry to say."

I persisted. "There's got to be something more we can do."

"How about we ask Quinn Walker the coroner to join us? He's just down the hall and is expecting to talk to you today. We might cover more ground more quickly if we're all here together." Olin picked up his phone.

Walker arrived so quickly that I wondered if he had been lurking in the hall. Olin made the introductions.

The coroner was middle-aged, overweight and slightly out of breath. He plopped into the remaining chair in the office and gave us a friendly smile. "I understand you folks have questions about the Hog Jaw shootings. What can I tell you?"

I began with the obvious question. "Do you have any thoughts on what might have happened? Are we looking at a mutual murder here? Or a murder/suicide?"

"Good question," Walker replied, but didn't elaborate.

I rephrased my question. "What can you tell us?" I asked. "How do you see this happening?"

Walker thought for a moment, then said, "A few of Jake Taylor's bullets went wild. One hit Lou Bancroft in the chest. That's what killed him. It appears that Bancroft fired only one shot, into Taylor's right temple. Taylor died instantaneously. Looks to me like Bancroft was a pretty good shot, since he fired at Taylor after taking a bullet himself. This suggests that Jake must've fired first, since Bancroft's shot was deadly."

"Could it be possible that Taylor shot Bancroft then turned the gun on himself?"

"I suppose," Olin admitted. "But we've got no way of knowing that."

Pete looked up. "Why not?"

"The stippling is inconclusive."

"The what?" Pete asked.

"Discoloration on the skin," Walker told him, "Caused by unspent gunpowder. This happens particularly with close-range gunshots. The more pronounced the stippling, the closer the shot. Our problem here is that the stippling on Taylor's head doesn't scream totally up close and personal, but it doesn't quite disprove it either."

Pete wasn't sure about that. "Why not?"

The coroner appeared on the verge of losing patience. "Because Jake had fairly long arms. He could have held the gun at arm's length and shot himself. Or it could have been Bancroft. It's a small room. He wasn't that far away."

The coroner stared at the ceiling, then added, "All we know for sure is that both men died from gunshot wounds. Wish I could be more helpful," he added.

So did I.

I wasn't about to give up yet. Turning to Olin, I asked, "What about the forensics results? Did you find anything interesting there?"

"Sadly, no," he replied. "We couldn't even test the bullet we removed from Jake. It shattered when it hit his head. As I said, the only thing we know for sure is that both men died from gunshot wounds. And the bullets we removed from Lou Bancroft's body most definitely came from the gun we found in Jake's hand."

"Did you run the fingerprints on both guns?"

Olin shook his head. "Why bother? After all, each of the victims died with a gun in his hand. That made it a no brainer, in my humble opinion."

I pressed on anyway. Doing my best to sound helpless and needy, I said, "My problem here is my boss. He's a stickler of the worst kind. He never lets me close a case if there's even the slightest hint of an unturned stone. And I need to close this case so Jake's widow can collect the insurance money. Could you do me a favor here and check the prints? To help Lillie Taylor?"

"When you put it like that," Olin sighed, "there's no way I can refuse you. Give me a day or two to run some tests. I'll get back to you with the results as soon as I can."

"That's all I can ask," I said. Then I immediately asked something else. "What about serial numbers on the guns? What did they show?"

The detective frowned. "Nothing helpful. The gun in Jake's hand was his own, all registered nice and legal. The serial number on Bancroft's gun had been removed—not completely, but just enough to make it useless."

Bummer. I hated dead ends. Then another thought occurred to me. "Did you check the rest of the motel room for prints as well?"

The sheriff nodded. "Always do. Standard operating procedure."

That was a relief.

"We didn't find anything of interest," he continued. "Plenty of Bancroft's prints, to be sure. A few of others as well. Ran them through the system. No results. I figured they probably belonged to the chambermaid."

That sounded reasonable, except that there was no chambermaid, only Lillie Taylor. "Thanks. I appreciate your time." I stood to leave.

The minute we were back in the car, Pete said, "That was brief. And to the point. Did you get anything useful out of it?"

"Perhaps," I told him. "But I'd like to hear your thoughts first."

"Hmmm. The coroner said it was the bullet to the brain that killed Jake, right?"

"Right," I said.

Pete continued, "Then either Bancroft is one hell of a good shot or Jake blew his own brains out. Logically, it could have gone either way."

"Exactly. It'll be interesting to check into Bancroft's background. Anything else?"

"That's it for the moment. Now I'd like to hear why you insisted on checking the guns for fingerprints. What are you thinking?"

"I'm not sure yet. I just have a hunch."

Chapter 11

Late Thursday morning

"What's up for the afternoon?" Pete asked me as we were driving out of Jackson.

"Back to Hog Jaw," I told him. "I'm meeting with one of the witnesses there. A local man named Chuck Andrews. I offered to buy him lunch while we talked, but he said no way would he eat at the Hog Jaw Diner. It might be interesting to learn why."

My phone rang before I could continue. Caller ID showed only a number, no name. "This is Amy Lynch," I said.

"Yeah, hi. This is Buster Dolan. I got a message that you wanted to speak with me. Something about the murders at the Hog Jaw Motel."

"That's right. I'm hoping you'll be available within the next few days. I'd appreciate getting a statement from you for my file."

"I'd be happy to help. But it'll have to be sometime today. I'm tied up the rest of the week and it's all stuff I can't change."

Luckily, my plans were more flexible. "How about this afternoon?" I suggested. "Can you meet me in Hog Jaw?"

He groaned. "That's a mighty long ride from where I am. Could we find someplace closer to me, like maybe half-way?"

Apparently I'd have to. "Hold on a sec. Let me look at a map." I futzed with my phone and pulled up a map of Tennessee. "Where are you now?"

"Just outside of Henderson," Dolan told me. "South of Jackson."

I scanned the map. "Aha!"

Pete turned and gave me a questioning look.

"That's not far from Pinson, right?" I asked. From what I could see, we were both around a half hour from the Pinson Mounds State Park.

"Uh, yeah. Right."

That was music to my ears. "Can you meet me there?"

"In Pinson?" Dolan asked.

"Yes. It looks to be a good half-way point. And this will give me a chance to visit the mounds. I've been wanting to do that for ages."

Dolan hesitated a few seconds. I could almost hear the wheels turning in his head. Finally he replied, "Yeah. Okay. Pinson it is. I can be there in about thirty minutes. I'll meet you in the parking lot just inside the entrance to the park. We can talk there. What are you driving?"

"A red Mustang convertible."

"Okay, then. See you there."

I smiled as I ended the call. Visiting the mounds would be a nice bonus. "This should be interesting," I said to Pete. "Some days things just go your way."

He pointed to the sky ahead. "It'd be more interesting if it weren't for those dark clouds rolling in from the west. It looks like we're about to get some rain. We better put the top up."

He pulled over to the side of the road to do so. Once safe from possible approaching rain, we resumed our ride to Pinson.

"What about that other guy you were supposed to speak with today in Hog Jaw?" Pete asked.

"Chuck Andrews. I'm calling him now to reschedule. He's local to the Hog Jaw area, so I'm guessing that won't be a problem for him."

"If he's local, why do you suppose he was staying at the Hog Jaw Motel on a Thursday night?" Pete asked.

I grinned. "I was wondering the same thing. My guess is that he was up to no good. At any rate, it should be interesting to hear what he has to say."

About 20 minutes later, I was all set to see Chuck Andrews on Friday. Pete and I pulled into the parking lot at the Pinson Mounds State Park and Museum. Interesting didn't begin to describe what greeted us. A massive mound off to the right dominated the view. Even in the rain, it took my breath away.

"Wow!" I said to Pete. "Can you feel it?"

"Feel what?"

"The atmosphere," I replied. "The aura. There's something in the air here. Something rather magical. Please tell me you can feel it."

"Huh?" was all he said.

I searched for the right words to explain myself. Finally, I told him, "It's a feeling of total peace, like being removed from the madness of everyday life. And being more connected to the earth … and all of its secrets."

Pete stopped the car and stared at me like I had taken leave of my senses. Finally he said, "Whatever you say, Ames." He pulled into a parking spot facing the mound.

"My poor prosaic Pete," I said to him. "Take a deep breath and soak in the surroundings. Maybe then you'll know what I mean."

Before he had a chance to respond to that, a car pulled up on the other side of the parking lot. A black mini-van, the stereotypical family vehicle. A weather-worn bumper sticker informed us "Baby on board." A shiny clean newer one simply said "Brave Hearts" in large red letters on a blue and white background.

A fellow got out of the van and walked toward our Mustang. He was thirty-ish and average in every way—neither tall nor short, brown hair, dark eyes, sun-tanned skin. He was dressed in beige khakis and a red plaid shirt, Titans baseball cap, whoever they were. He looked more like an accountant than a biker - no leather jacket, no boots or torn jeans. No long white pony tail. No tricked-out Harley. What was up with that?

It seemed that Pete was wondering the same thing. "This guy's a biker?" he asked.

"What can I tell you? I guess everybody has some sort of alter-ego."

"Ms. Lynch?" the fellow asked as he knocked on the passenger side window.

"Yes." I exited the car and offered my hand to him. "Buster Dolan?"

He shook my outstretched hand. "The one and only. Nice to meet you."

"Likewise," I said. "Please call me Amy. And this is my associate, Pete Devereaux," I said as Pete got out of the Mustang.

Dolan nodded at Pete. "A pleasure. Sorry about the rain, though. Do you folks have an umbrella?"

I shook my head. "Rental cars don't come with them." I pointed to the museum building. "Perhaps we better go inside before we all get drenched to the bone. It's beginning to come down pretty hard." I was well aware that we could talk in his car. We wouldn't fit well in the Mustang. The thing was, I really wanted to see the museum.

Dolan frowned. "Yeah. I suppose we'll have to." He pulled his baseball cap down further over his forehead.

The three of us made a quick dash to the museum door. An elderly man, tall and thin as a rail, greeted us inside. He had long gray hair, braided and beaded, and weathered skin. My best guess was that he was Native American.

"Hello, folks. Welcome to Pinson. I'm Joseph Wakhan, caretaker of the mounds, also the local shaman. Please feel free to have a look around." He gave us a big semi-toothless smile, took a long, slow look at Buster Dolan, then added "I'll be nearby if you have any questions."

"So, what can I do for you folks?" Dolan asked. "I understand you have some questions about the recent events in Hog Jaw. Such a tragedy." He gave us an appropriately sad frown. I hoped it was genuine.

I pulled out my phone. "Do you mind if I tape this?"

"Feel free."

I did. "You were at the Hog Jaw Motel the night of the shooting?"

"Correct," he said, but didn't elaborate.

"Do you visit there often?"

"Sure do. That's home base for my buddies and me. Pretty much every weekend, weather permitting. We're a motorcycle club of sorts. Really just a bunch of guys letting off steam on the weekends. The area around Hog Jaw is great for riding."

"I see. I was led to believe the shooting took place on a Thursday night."

"Right."

Time to get a little nosey. "What brought you there during the week?"

Dolan looked past me, out the window that looked out on the big mound. "Business. It happens every once in a while. If the job brings me out that way, I usually stay in Hog Jaw, particularly if it's late in the day. I like it there. Clean rooms, low rates, nice friendly people. It sure beats driving all the way to Henderson in the dark, or if I'm over-tired."

"What business are you in?" Pete asked.

"Software development," Dolan replied. "I won't bore you with the details."

"Please tell me what happened that night," I said. "What you heard and saw. Any little detail could be important."

Dolan frowned as he thought. "There's really nothing much to tell. I was sleeping. Lillie's screams woke me up. That and the sirens."

"Does that mean you didn't hear a noise earlier?" I asked. "Maybe something that sounded like a truck back-firing?"

"Sorry. I'm usually a pretty sound sleeper. And back-firing trucks are so common I hardly even notice them anymore."

So far, that was less than helpful. I forged on, hoping he'd have something of interest to contribute. "What did you do when you heard the commotion?"

"Threw on some clothes and went outside to see what was happening."

"What did you see?"

"Well, let me think. There was an ambulance just arriving, and a couple of cop cars. Lillie was shaking and crying. The sheriff was doing what he could to calm her down." Dolan paused for a moment. "And that's about it."

There had to be something more. "There was another biker there as well, right?"

"Yeah. That was Miller, Gary Miller."

"Were you two there together?" Pete asked.

Dolan shook his head. "Nope. Both just happened to be in the area. Like I said, I had business nearby. Gary was on his way to Nashville to see his brother. We had dinner together at the diner, then went our separate ways."

"Was there anybody else around?"

Dolan shrugged. "Yeah. A guy I've seen there a couple of times. He usually has a woman with him. Didn't see her that night, though."

This was the first I'd heard about a woman. "Do you know who she is?"

"Nope. But I'm guessing she's not his wife."

"Why is that? Pete asked.

Dolan gave that some thought. "I guess it's because the two of them come and go in separate vehicles. And they never eat in the diner, not even breakfast."

That sounded reasonable. Where better not to be seen than in Hog Jaw? "Did you speak with anybody the night of the shootings?" I asked.

"Just the sheriff. He took my information, asked me a few questions. No big deal, really. He told me to be available if anything else came up. I said I would, then went back to my room. Better to stay out of the way, if you know what I mean."

I paused to regroup my thoughts. "Were you acquainted with Jake Taylor?"

"Yes and no. I saw him around the place often enough, doing chores and whatnot. I usually do business with Lillie, though. From what I can see, she runs the place."

"What about Lou Bancroft, the other man who was killed?" I asked. "Did you know him?"

"Is that his name?"

"Yes, it is," I said.

"If he's the guy I'm thinking he is, I believe I saw him around once or twice, probably in the diner."

"Did you ever speak with him?"

Dolan shook his head. "Don't believe I did."

"Is there anything else you can tell us?" I asked, ever-hopeful.

He shook his head again. "I'm afraid not. Guess I'm not much help. Sorry to drag you all the way out here for nothing."

I glanced across the room. A younger man who appeared to be indigenous had joined the caretaker. They were speaking softly and looking in our direction.

Dolan looked at his watch. "I really better be going now. You've got my number if anything else comes up."

He dashed out the door before I even had a chance to thank him.

Chapter 12

Late Thursday morning

I turned to Pete as we watched Buster Dolan disappear from sight. "Was it something I said?"

Before Pete could respond, Joseph Wakhan, aka the shaman and caretaker of the mounds, approached us. "I regret that your friend had to leave so soon," Wakhan said. "Pity. Our museum may be small, but it has a lot to offer. These mounds have a rich and fascinating history."

"I'm sure they do," I answered. "I learned a little about them in school. It's wonderful to have the opportunity to see them in person."

"I hope they live up to your expectations," he said. "This rain is regrettable, although even foul weather can't obscure the grandeur of our mounds."

"The sheer size of that one out there is amazing," Pete said. "Are they all that large?"

Wakhan shook his head. "What you see there is the largest of the mounds. It is approximately 100 feet tall. There are 14 more mounds spread out over the 1,200 acres of our park here. They come in a variety of shapes and sizes."

"Who built them?" Pete asked.

I was tempted to answer him, but deferred to the shaman.

"The local indigenous peoples. My ancestors. Over 2,000 years ago."

Pete let out a long, low whistle. "Wow. That's old and then some. What were they used for?"

"They had a variety of purposes," the shaman said. "Some were burial mounds. Others were ceremonial. The mounds here at Pinson were particularly important for native ceremonies, mostly due to their location. They were relatively central to many of the original inhabitants of North America. People from all over the continent came here for the summer meetings and rituals. Relics have been found in the area which have been proven to come from as far away as what is now called Idaho."

"What kind of relics?" Pete asked.

"Mostly shards of pottery," the shaman answered. "Pottery differs considerably from one region, from one tribe, to another. It was quite obvious that many of the pottery shards and other items found here originated elsewhere."

I was thoroughly enjoying watching Pete show some interest in the mounds. And Shaman Wakhan appeared to be delighting in his audience. Nevertheless, I felt more than a few pangs of guilt about taking time away from my case. I was pretty sure Mark wouldn't approve. Still I made no move to hurry things along. I'd work harder later to make up for the time—or some such thing. "It must be wonderful to be the caretaker of such a magical place," I said to Wakhan.

Pete gave me a sideways glance as he often did when he heard me use the word "magical." As usual, I ignored it.

A sad smile dashed across the shaman's face. "You are correct," he said to me. "This place is indeed magical. It is a privilege and an honor to be in my position as caretaker. Sadly, it is also a burden. I am an old man and there is much that needs to be done, both here and elsewhere, to honor and preserve our heritage."

As he said this, the younger fellow I had seen enter the museum earlier walked over to us.

"This is my grandson Thomas," Wakhan said. "He is my helper. Eventually he will take over my duties as caretaker, and shaman as well. The job is becoming larger than my ability to perform it."

"It's nice to meet you," Thomas said. "And an honor to be of assistance to my grandfather."

"And I wish you well in your position," I told him. "These mounds and the civilization they represent are an important part of our heritage."

Thomas grinned broadly.

I turned to the old shaman. "A minute ago, you said there is much to do both here and elsewhere. Are there other mounds in the area which you oversee as well?"

"Indeed there are," he replied. "There is a small mound just outside of Humboldt. It is close by and still in good shape. That is not a problem. Sadly, the mound in Hog Jaw is a different story."

That sounded like a story I wanted to hear. "In Hog Jaw?" I said. "That's where we're staying. At the Hog Jaw Motel."

"Then you may have seen this mound," Thomas said. "If you have ventured to the top of Hog Jaw Mountain."

"We've explored part of the mountain," Pete said, "but have not yet been to the top."

Thomas' eyes clouded over. "It is a sad sight at present. The mound has fallen into disrepair through no fault of ours."

"How so?" I asked.

"Traffic in that area has increased considerably in recent years," Wakhan said. "Both from vehicles on the road and the increasing numbers of people using the footpaths."

"Are you talking about hikers exploring the area?" I asked.

"In part," Wakhan replied. "There are also the motorcyclists who use the area for their weekend rides. It is difficult to stop them. And there is ever-increasing traffic from the people at Armstrong Industries. As their company grows, their use of the land does as well."

"Who owns the land?" Pete asked.

"We do," replied Thomas. "Our people. Although the county would tell you otherwise. We never recognized their claim. This was a matter of contention for many years. Eventually, we have come to a compromise of sorts. We have agreed not to contest the use of hiking paths on the lower part of the mountain. The county has agreed to allow us exclusive use of the area at the top, where the mound is. In the past year or so, others have sought to purchase even this small area from us for purposes of their own. We cannot let this happen. The mound is sacred to our people. To turn it over to strangers would be a sacrilege."

I couldn't argue with that. "I wish you all the best with that," I said.

It was time to change the subject. "Could you show us around the museum?" I asked.

The old shaman's face lit up. "It would be my pleasure to do so."

We spent the next hour with Joseph Wakhan learning the history and mystery of the Pinson Mounds. By then, the rain had stopped, so we were able to venture outside and climb the seemingly endless staircase to the top of the largest mound. The view made it worth the effort. And despite Pete's disbelief, it was indeed magical.

On the drive back to Hog Jaw, Pete said to me, "I really enjoyed that. It was fascinating. Did you learn anything that might help your case?"

"I think perhaps I did."

"And what was that?"

"I learned I'd like to know more about what goes on on Hog Jaw Road."

Chapter 13

Late Thursday afternoon

I touched base with Peggy at the office on the ride back to Hog Jaw. Having a chauffeur came in pretty handy at times.

"Hello to you," Peggy greeted me in her usually cheery way. "I'm so glad you called."

Uh oh. "Why is that? Did something happen?"

"No. Nothing. And that's the problem. Things are deadly dull around here," she told me. "I don't know how much longer I can stand it."

"Not enough work to keep you busy?" I asked.

I heard a long, sad sigh. "There's plenty to do. The trouble is that every bit of it is the same old routine. I'm hungry for a more exotic claim, or at least something more interesting than a dented fender or a chimney fire."

"I get what you're saying. Nevertheless, the powers that be give us money to deal with these mundane tasks, and so we do."

"At least until something more interesting comes along," Peggy said. "And I do keep hoping."

"As boring as life may be at the moment, are you at least able to keep up with things? Do you need some help?" I asked her. although I doubted that would ever be the case.

"I'm doing fine. Tiffany has been helping me push the never-ending paper. She's here now. For some unknown reason, George isn't on her case at the moment. Maybe he found a new hobby. Or somebody else to pick on. I'll put the phone on speaker."

"Hello Tiff," I said. "As always, we appreciate your assistance."

"My pleasure," she said. "I'm always happy to get away from George for a while."

Peggy spoke up, "Having Tiffany here to help has given me more time to do the research you asked for."

I perked up. "Please tell me it's about Armstrong Industries."

"You bet it is."

"And?" I put my phone in my lap and grabbed a pen and notebook from my purse. Wished there was a way to set my phone to record when I was on a call. Perhaps there was and I just didn't know about it. At the moment, though, I wasn't in the mood to try. Some things are far more important than being technologically adept.

"Here's the scoop," Peggy began. "The company was founded in 1997 by a small group of ex-military folks. From the Gulf war era. Most of the 78 current employees come from the same background. I guess that makes some sense. You know, soldiers, bombs, weapons of mass destruction. They somehow go together. Anyway, Armstrong Industries occupies five buildings on 1200 acres of land in the boondocks of West Tennessee. That's a good thing. Makes it safer if there were ever an accident, which there has never been, yet. So far, their safety record is spotless. As you know, their largest client is the Department of Defense. Other customers include a couple dozen mining, blasting and commercial demolition businesses, which all sounds reasonable. That is not to mention a surprising amount of sales to some foreign military and police forces. That last part makes me more than a little uncomfortable, but from what I could find, it hasn't been a problem yet."

That was a relief.

"And I'm afraid that's all the information there is on Armstrong," Peggy said. "I had been hoping for something more intriguing. Sorry."

"Actually, bombs are pretty intriguing," I said. "Still, I suppose I better keep my attention focused on my case. Mark doesn't like it much when I spend the company's time going down rabbit holes."

Tiffany laughed. "So what can we do for you today? Please tell us that you're looking for information on someone or something at least as interesting as bombs."

"There are two things at the moment," I told them. "First of all, can you see what you can find on the Brave Hearts?"

"Brave Hearts?" Tiffany repeated. "Is that a group or association of some kind? Maybe some Scottish bagpipers?"

I giggled at the thought. "At this point, I'm not sure. I saw the name on a bumper sticker today, on a car belonging to a witness I was interviewing. For all I know, it could be the name of a kid's little league baseball team or the local high school football squad. But it can't hurt to look into it."

"You've got it," Peggy said. "If there's anything of interest going on with the Brave Hearts, you can count on us to find it for you."

"And what's the other subject to research?" Tiffany asked.

"You're going to love this one, Tiffany," I told her. "Please see what you can learn about the Shaman Joseph Wakhan and his grandson Thomas. They're both part of the tribe that maintains the Pinson Mounds."

"What's a shaman?" Peggy asked.

"What are you, new?" Tiffany said. "You really don't know?"

"Sorry," Peggy said. "I've led a sheltered life. At least until now."

"In many Native American cultures, a shaman is part medicineman, part priest. They're powerful people. Well-respected. Some people say they're somewhat magical as well. That should be interesting to research," Tiffany said. "I'll get right on it."

"Thanks," I said. "Now to the really important question. How's my friend Sam doing, Peggy?"

"He's the best dog ever," she said. "Even though I'm sure he misses you, he and I are having a wonderful time together."

"So he's behaving himself?" I asked.

"As he always does," Peggy replied.

"Give him a big hug and a doggie treat for me."

"Will do. And how's Pete?"

"Pete's fine," I responded.

"That's right," Pete chimed in. "Just living the dream here in West Tennessee."

We pulled up to the Hog Jaw Motel. "Gotta go," I told my co-workers. "It's time to get back to business. Wish me luck."

Chapter 14

Early Thursday evening

Lillie Taylor and her sister Noreen were outside the door to the motel office, carrying what I assumed to be Lillie's bags inside. "Hello, Ladies," I said. "Are you moving back in, Lillie? And re-opening the motel?"

Lillie grinned. "I sure am. And just in time for the weekend. It's a big relief not to lose that business. I really need the money. Property taxes are going to be due soon and there are a few rooms that need some sprucing up, and a few bathrooms that could use an update. It never ends."

I thought it was probably good to see her looking ahead.

"Noreen will be staying with me for a while," Lillie continued. "At least until I get my act together and figure out what to do next."

"You're lucky to have her," Pete said.

Lillie nodded.

The look on Noreen's face didn't exactly scream "lucky."

Lillie checked us in, showing Noreen how it was done in the process.

As Pete and I dropped our bags off in our room, I looked around and groaned as quietly as I could. Once again, there was only one bed, a double. I'd have to deal with it somehow, hopefully later rather than sooner. I'd find a way to make it all right.

At the moment, I was acutely aware of how hungry I was. I had been so wrapped up in my meetings with Joseph Wakhan the shaman and Buster Dolan the biker that I had completely forgotten about eating lunch. Highly atypical behavior for me. Pete and I could unpack and settle in to the room later. At the moment, my stomach was calling out to me - loudly. We made our way to the Hog Jaw Diner post haste.

The place was hopping, despite the early hour. It seemed that 5:00 PM might be the usual dinner hour in these parts. Walt Taylor greeted us at the door like old friends. "Welcome back. It's nice to see you folks again." He looked around the crowded room, then led us to a table for two in the rear of the room.

"What's good tonight?" Pete asked.

"Beef stew or baked chicken with gravy. And cornbread." Walt told us. "Best cornbread for miles around."

"That's for sure," I said. "I think I'll have the beef stew. And a glass of Pinot Noir, if you have it. A large glass."

"That sounds good to me," Pete said. "I'll have the same, except with a beer. That IPA I had the other day was pretty good."

"Coming right up." Walt left to put in our order. When he returned with our wine and beer, Pete asked him, "Are you usually this busy so early on a Thursday evening?"

Walt grinned from ear to ear. "We didn't used to be, but lately times have changed for the better. Business-wise at least. It's good. Helps us deal with everything else life slings at us." He looked around the room as if surveying his kingdom.

"Any idea why the increase in business?" I asked.

"I don't know. Maybe it's the cornbread."

Minnie approached the table carrying our beef stew and corn-bread. "Here you go, folks. Enjoy." She didn't stick around to chat, didn't even try to smile. I couldn't blame her.

Pete and I dug into our meals with great enthusiasm. As we ate, I surveyed the room. Most of the tables were filled. And with a variety of characters. There were some weary-looking middle-aged men sitting at the counter staring at their food. My best guess was that they were truckers. A few tables were occupied by what appeared to be young lovers. Who knew that Thursday was date night in Tennessee?

Two tables in the front of the room each held one lone occupant, each a forty-ish overweight man wearing faded jeans and in need of a shave and a shampoo. The remainder of the room consisted of two groups of men, three at one table, four at another, all very well-groomed and busi-ness-like. These fellows were dressed like the ones we'd seen before - kha-kis and blue shirts with a logo on them. They may have been the same guys we had seen the other day. They definitely worked for Armstrong Indus-tries. I wished I could get close enough to eavesdrop on their conversation. No particular reason, actually. I was just curious what folks who made bombs talked about at dinner. I decided that it probably wasn't a good idea to appear overly nosey. Instead, I simply ordered dessert.

As we waited for our homemade apple pie to arrive, I said to Pete, "Could you do something for me?"

"What's that?" he asked.

"Go to the Men's Room."

His eyes filled with disbelief. "What did you say?"

"I said, will you please go to the Men's Room. It's important."

Pete dropped his fork onto the table and stared at me. "And why, exactly, is it so important? To you, I mean."

"It's a reconnaissance mission. And one I can't do myself."

"In the Men's Room? What is going on in that head of yours?"

"Curiosity is going on," I told him. "I couldn't help but notice that's there's a lot of men's restroom traffic this evening. We've been here less than an hour. In that time, both of those scruffy-looking guys have gone in there, one of them twice. And a couple of the men in the blue shirts have been in and out as well. It makes me wonder what could possibly be the attraction."

Pete gave that some thought. "Other than the usual reasons, you mean? Perhaps a stomach bug going around? Or do you think they're selling drugs in there or something?"

"That's what I'm looking to find out. So, please, humor me."

He sighed mightily, but did as I asked. Returning a few minutes later, he shook his head and said, "Nothing untoward happening in there from what I could see. Just the usual Men's Room—one stall, two urinals and a sink. A couple of guys were on their way out when I went in, one in jeans, the other in khakis. Seemed like business as usual."

Maybe, I thought. Or maybe not.

Chapter 15

Thursday evening

Back in our room, I took a good look around. It was pretty much the standard older motel motif—previously-noted double bed with a faded quilt and a few too many pillows, mismatched end tables with matching lamps, a bureau/desk with an oversized TV on top, a mini fridge. The place was a little old, and a little tired, but it was spotlessly clean. Pete and I would be comfortable enough here. And it couldn't hurt my investigation to be where the action was—or at least where it had been.

Pete hung a few of his things in the closet and dumped the rest into a drawer. "I'm looking forward to a nice relaxing evening together," he said. "It'll give us plenty of time to talk. We really need to do that, you know." He sat on the edge of the bed and gave me what could only be described as a hopeful smile.

"Right," I replied. "Of course we do. But first I need to do a little work—check my emails, make a few notes, review the information I've got so far on my investigation. Is that all right with you?"

"I guess it'll have to be," he sighed, then flopped down onto the bed and turned on the television—just a little bit too loud.

I did my best to tune out the background noise from the television, set my laptop up on the desk and got to work. After adding notes on what

I had seen, heard, and learned during the day, I pulled up the photos I had taken of room 8. It was time to study the scene of the crime. One by one, I enlarged each photo and pored over every detail, no matter how small. I compared the room in the photos to my own room. Other than some blood stains and bullet holes, they were virtually identical, right down to the faded quilts and mis-matched end tables. Nothing at all helpful, or so it seemed.

I double-checked the forensic report on what had been found in room 8. I compared that information to the photos, asking myself if anything may have been missed. Nothing leapt out at me. I closed my eyes, took a few deep breaths, and did my damndest to clear my mind. Then I opened my eyes, stared at the photos again, and gazed around my room. I got up and walked around, took a quick look out into the parking area, double-checked that the door was locked. Anything I could think of to occupy my conscious mind and hoped that my subconscious would kick in. I sighed and sat back down.

A few things hit me all at once. The door! Had the forensic team checked that for fingerprints as well, knobs and all? Surely Lillie's prints were there, but were there any others? And what about the lights? Lillie said they were off when she opened the door, which made no sense at all. Who turned them off? Did whoever it was leave any fingerprints? And the windows? Lillie told me that she had opened them to air out the room. They were closed in the photos. Did Lillie do that? Or Lou Bancroft? Was it the police? Or somebody else? Somebody with fingers.

I jumped up so quickly I knocked most of my notes onto the floor. "I've got to go out for a few minutes, Pete," I said. "I'll be back shortly." I dashed out the door so fast I didn't even hear his response.

I hurried over to the motel office. Lillie and Noreen were both behind the desk looking at some paperwork. "Well hello there," Lillie said with a smile. "Is everything all right? Is your room okay? Can I do something for you?"

"I have a quick question or two," I told her. "If you have the time."

"Sure," Lillie said.

Noreen's scowl suggested otherwise. "Really? Do you really have to do this now? Couldn't it wait until morning? Can't you see we're busy here? We have a business we're trying to run."

"It will only take a minute," I told her.

"And what's the problem anyway?" Noreen continued. "You're not trying to accuse Lillie of anything, are you?"

Odd thing for her to ask. I shook my head. "I'm just looking to clear up a few minor facts. It's nothing to worry about. Truly."

Noreen glared at me.

Lillie finally found her tongue. "It's all right, Noreen," she said. "I can answer her questions." Turning to me, she asked, "What do you want to know?"

"When we spoke the other day, you told me you're the person who cleans the rooms. Is that right?"

She nodded. "Right."

"And you cleaned room 8 in the afternoon after Lou Bancroft called to tell you he was on his way."

"Right again."

"Did you do a real thorough cleaning?" I asked. I knew I was pressing a point there, but it could be important.

"Always. Why do you ask?" Lillie responded.

Noreen spoke up. "Are you saying that there was something wrong? Something not done properly? The room wasn't clean enough?"

"No, not at all," I replied. "I just need to confirm a few details. Lillie, did you wipe down the door knobs and the light switches?"

"Of course I did," Lillie told me. "With disinfectant. The same as I always do. Why? Is that important?"

"It could be," I told her. "What about the windows? You told me you opened them to air the room out. Did you close them when you left?"

She thought about that for a moment, then shook her head. "Actually no. It was a lovely warm day so I decided to leave them open. Lou could close them if later if he wanted to."

"Thanks. That's helpful. I'll let you get back to your work now. Good night."

A variety of thoughts bumped around in my head as I walked back into the room. First and foremost, was Lillie telling me the truth? Might she be keeping something from me? If so, why? As much as I hated to admit it, she hardly came across as the grieving widow.

I wasn't sure I bought the police's mutual shoot-out theory. It was simply too improbable that both men could pull that off no matter how many bullets they fired. And where, when or how had Jake gotten hold of his gun anyway? Based on what Lillie told me, it was missing.

One other question remained unanswered: Who turned out the lights in room 8?

I was so distracted by that thought that I wandered off of the walkway and into the parking lot. Once there, I failed to notice a vehicle pulling in. Apparently the driver was distracted as well. He slammed on his brakes with a screech and narrowly avoided hitting me. As I was catching my breath and listening to my heart thumping in my chest, the driver opened his window and said, "Sorry about that, Lady. I didn't see you."

I was too shaken to answer him. I was also damned if I was going to say "Oh, that's all right. No harm done. I'm fine" - or anything else equally wimpy. I shook my head by way of acknowledgement then stepped back with a sweeping hand gesture to let him pass.

As he pulled ahead, I took a good look at his vehicle, mainly so I could avoid it in the future. A dark colored mini-van, like you see everywhere in suburban America. It did, however, have one distinguishing feature—a bumper sticker that said Brave Hearts. Either this fellow was from the same town as Buster Dolan or the Brave Hearts were something more wide-spread than just a local sports team. I was more eager than ever to see what Peggy would turn up on them.

I returned to the room to find Pete sound asleep and snoring loudly, the television still blaring. It looked like our heart-to-heart talk would have to wait. I was dog tired and still needed to update my notes before going to bed. Pete would understand. At least I hoped he would.

Chapter 16

Friday morning

I lay in bed in the morning pretending I was still asleep. Pete had snuggled up close to me some time in the night. I had done my best not to notice. Now, opening my eyes would mean I had to face Pete and I wasn't sure I was ready to do so. He wanted to have a serious talk when I was heading out to speak with Lillie last night. I put him off. I could have roused him when I returned to the room. I probably should have done so. Instead, I managed to convince myself that the poor guy was really tired and needed his beauty sleep. It was most likely a lie. I sucked in a big breath and prepared myself to deal with the consequences.

Apparently Pete had other ideas. He rolled over and greeted me with a big smile. "Good morning, Ames," he said. "Time to rise and shine. It looks like it's going to be yet another beautiful day."

Some days you just live right. I knew this cheery mood was only a reprieve, but I'd take it for now. We could deal with our issues once my case was over. I always was somewhat of a coward where personal relationships were concerned. And sadly aware that this was nothing to be proud of.

"What's on your agenda this morning?" he asked. "Anything wild and crazy?"

"I wish. Unfortunately, it's just business as usual. I'm meeting with a witness after breakfast. Local fellow who was here the night Jake died. With any luck, he'll have something interesting to offer. Then Sheriff Snow is coming out to finish up in room 8. I want to take a look at a few things in there while I have the chance. Will you be joining me?"

He shook his head. "Actually, no. It's too beautiful a morning to spend inside. I'm curious to locate the mound that Shaman Wakham told us about. He said it's at the top of Hog Jaw Mountain."

"Will you be needing the car?" That could present a problem. I had no idea what might crop up in the course of the day.

"No," he replied. "I'll take a hike there. I found a path out behind the motel that leads through the woods to Hog Jaw Road. And the exercise will do me good."

"That sounds nice," I said. "I wish I could join you."

Pete stared at his feet. After a slightly uncomfortable silence, he said "To tell you the truth, I think it's better for me to go there by myself. I need a little alone time to do some thinking. You understand, right?"

"Sure," I said, wishing that I didn't.

We had a quick breakfast at the diner. Pete left without finishing his scrambled eggs. I ate everything on my plate, then hung around outside the diner waiting for Chuck Andrews. For reasons he chose not to share with me, he didn't want to meet me inside the Hog Jaw Diner. Instead, he said he'd pick me up out front and we could drive around somewhere while we talked. Odd, but what could I do? I needed to speak with the man.

I felt less than proud of myself as I gazed across the parking lot watching Pete head off. Way down deep, I knew I wasn't being fair to him but I continued to avoid dealing with it. Then a voice in the parking lot called me back into the moment. "Ms. Lynch? Good morning. I'm Chuck Andrews."

I turned to see a bright shiny new white Mustang convertible, with the top down, pull up in front of the diner. Here was a man after my own heart. "Yes. Hello. It's nice to meet you, Mr. Andrews. I love your car."

He broke into a large grin. "Thanks. So do I. It was a birthday gift from my wife. And please call me Chuck."

"You're a lucky man, Chuck," I told him. "to deserve a gift like this."

"Please, get in. Make yourself comfortable."

That was easy to do. Mustangs always felt right.

"I hope you're fine with the top down," Chuck said.

I smiled at him as I fastened my seat belt. "I wouldn't have it any other way, particularly on a morning like this. Early spring sunshine should never be wasted. Thank you so much for agreeing to meet with me. Witnesses are always such a critical part of my investigations."

He nodded by way of acknowledgement. "Let's take a ride while we talk. There's a little country road not far from here. Nice scenery, and you hardly ever see another car."

"Works for me."

Chuck pulled out from the diner parking lot and turned the car toward the road which led to the Snuggle Inn. It was the same road Pete and I had come in on from the airport. The road where we'd spotted Armstrong Industries. As I recalled, we hadn't seen any other cars then either.

I studied Chuck as we drove away from Hog Jaw. He was a well-dressed fifty-something man trying his darndest to look thirty-five. It didn't quite work. The slight paunch and the graying hair gave him away. He also overdid it just a bit on the aftershave. I was glad the top was down.

"So you want to talk with me about the incident last Thursday night at the Hog Jaw Motel," he began.

"That's correct." I pulled out my phone. "Do you mind if I record this?"

He hesitated, then finally said, "I guess that's okay, But I do have one request, if you don't mind."

"What's that?"

He stared at the road ahead. "Well, I'd appreciate it if you could keep it quiet that I was at the motel that night."

I sprung to attention. "Why is that?"

"Well, um, the thing is, my wife doesn't know that I was there. She thinks I was in Nashville. On business. I'm in sales."

He didn't specify what he sold. Oh well. "I see. Do you want to tell me why you were in Hog Jaw when you were allegedly in Nashville?" *Or would you like me to guess? I could come up with some pretty fun scenarios.*

Chuck swallowed hard. "Well, you see, I wasn't there alone."

I kept silent, waiting for him to explain himself.

After a slightly uncomfortable couple of moments, he said, "And I wasn't with my wife."

No surprise there. "Oh?" was all I said.

"Yeah. The thing is, I was with a friend. A lady friend."

"I see." I waited for more.

"My wife doesn't know about her. I'd prefer to keep it that way."

I felt a surge of pity for the woman who had given him a Mustang convertible. Chuck's attitude toward her lowered him in my estimation. Doing my best to sound casual, I told him, "Not to worry. Your secret is safe with me." *Unless, of course, it affects my case. And even then, I'd do my best not to out you.* "I will, however, need to have your friend's name. I will probably want to speak with her."

He groaned. "I was afraid of that, though I guess I can't blame you." After a few moments of tortured silence, he added, "Her name is Olivia. Olivia Franklin. She lives in Humboldt. And I'm pretty sure she didn't see or hear anything."

We'd see about that. In the meantime, I tapped the recorder button on my phone. I did a brief intro of time, place and who was speaking, then asked," What room were you in?"

"Room 1," he said. "Same as usual."

"Please tell me what happened that night. What you saw and heard. Anything you can remember could be helpful."

Chuck turned into the Armstrong Industries driveway and turned the Mustang around, heading back toward Hog Jaw. And perhaps buying some time to think?

"It was a little after 11:00," he began. "I was just drifting off to sleep when I heard a woman screaming. I jumped out of bed, threw on some clothes and grabbed my phone. I ran out the door. Lillie was there, in front of the room at the end. She was screaming and crying something terrible."

Lillie, is it? So she and Chuck were on a first name basis. That probably meant that he was a regular customer. He and his friend Olivia. Oh well, not my place to judge.

Chuck continued, "I ran over to see if I could help Lillie. Did my best to comfort her and to find out what was going on. The poor woman was hysterical, and not making a lot of sense. All I could make out was that somebody was dead. I called Emmet Snow, you know, the sheriff. He told me to stay with Lillie and keep her calm until he got there. And not to let her, or anybody else, into that room. He'd get there are fast as he could. Him and an ambulance."

"That must have been very upsetting for you," I said. "What happened next?"

"I did like Emmet asked. A few other guests had come out of their rooms by then as well. I told them help was on the way and they should stay where they were. Sheriff Stone's car pulled up shortly, with an ambulance right behind it. Emmet asked us all to remain where we were until he could take statements from us."

"Did you speak with any of the other guests?" I asked.

Chuck shook his head. "No. Just told them to stick around."

"Did you know any of them?"

"Not exactly. I'd seen a few of them a time or two in the parking lot. I don't know that we ever actually spoke or anything."

"What happened next?"

"Everybody waited outside for a bit, then Emmet and Lucas, his deputy, took our statements. After that, we all went back into our rooms, trying to keep out of the Sheriff's way. Nobody really wanted to get involved."

That jived with what sheriff Snow told me. Always a plus in my business.

"Where was your friend Olivia while all this was going on?" I had to ask.

He frowned. "I had told her to stay in the room. But when I got back there, she was gone. Must have slipped away when nobody was looking in her direction."

I couldn't say that I blamed the woman for that. I nodded, realized Chuck couldn't see a nod while he was driving, and said, "I will need a contact number for your friend Olivia."

He recited the number to me from memory. I repeated it slowly into my phone, then asked, "Did you know Jake Taylor?"

"Only to say hello to. I usually dealt with Lillie."

Usually? I guessed that confirmed that Andrews was a regular guest at the motel. "What about Lou Bancroft, the other fellow who was killed? Did you know him?"

"Not really," Chuck replied. "If he's the one I think he is, I'd seen him around a couple of times. I guess Hog Jaw was on his regular truck route. We probably said hello once or twice. Nothing more than that."

"Is there anything else you can think of?" I asked.

Chuck took a minute to think that over. Finally, he replied, "Nope. I'm afraid not. Nothing else comes to mind."

I turned off my recording. "Thank you so much for your help. If I think of anything else, I'll give you a call."

"Sure," he said. "Why not?" After a moment, he added, "Are you going to get in touch with Olivia now?"

"I have to. It's part of the job. But don't worry. Your secret is safe with me." *At least for now.*

Chapter 17

Friday, Mid-morning

Chuck dropped me off in the Hog Jaw Motel parking lot. I checked the room. No sign of Pete. I guessed that meant that he was still out enjoying his hike on Hog Jaw Mountain. That was fine with me. I needed to concentrate on my case. And his presence had a way of distracting me. Now was not the time for that, particularly with the odd mood he was in.

As soon as Chuck pulled out, I phoned his lady friend Olivia Franklin. If she was at the motel the night of the shootings, she could have seen something of interest. I got a busy signal. Left a message.

A police car pulled up in front of room 8. Sheriff Snow and a tall, lanky man also in uniform got out. "Morning, Ms. Lynch," Snow said with a smile. "Nice to see you again. This here is Officer Graham from the State Police tech lab in Jackson."

Officer Graham acknowledged my presence with a nod, but not even a hint of a smile. Oh well. I didn't need to spend much time with the man.

"I really appreciate you folks coming out here again," I told them. "I wouldn't be able to close this claim without you."

"We're happy to help," Snow said.

Officer Graham didn't look so happy to me. He cleared his throat. A bit too loudly. "How about we get started on this errand so I can get back to Jackson sometime this morning? I've got a lot of important work waiting for me there."

I decided not to remind him that this job was work as well, not to mention important. "Sounds good. Here's what I need. Please do a thorough check for prints on all of the door knobs, light switches, also the curtain pulls and the windows."

"Windows?" Graham asked. "What's with them?"

"Somebody closed them. I need to know who. Please dust anywhere a person might touch windows, the glass included. Then we'll need to get Lillie's prints as well."

Snow's eyes opened wide. "Whatever for?"

"So we can eliminate them," I told him.

"And where might we find this Lillie?" Graham asked.

"She'll be in the motel office." I said.

Snow's face perked up. "She's back from Noreen's?"

"Yes. She returned yesterday, right after speaking with you. It was important to her to get the motel reopened right away."

"Is she alone?" he asked.

"No. Noreen is with her."

A look of relief dashed across Snow's face. "That's good to hear. Lillie really shouldn't be alone at a time like this. Noreen gets a little high and mighty sometimes, like she's the only one who know what's best—about everything. But she has always been good to Lillie. Protective. Lillie needs that right now."

He started to say something further. Graham interrupted. "Guess I'll get started in the room now. Can you unlock the door for me?"

Snow didn't join Officer Graham in room 8. Perhaps he preferred my company to Graham's.

I decided a little small talk might be nice. "So, tell me, Sheriff, do you live far from here? Do you have a family?"

He shook his head. "No wife. No family."

"Oh?" I asked, curious to hear more. I couldn't help it. Being nosy was in my bones.

"Yeah. Guess I never found the right woman," he said, a faraway look in his eyes.

I wondered if he was still carrying a torch for Lillie after all this time.

Snow checked his watch, then changed the subject. "So, tell me, how's your case going? Making good progress?" he asked.

"I'm getting there, slowly but surely." This wasn't exactly true, but if I said it aloud perhaps I could make it so.

"Anything I can help you with?" Snow asked.

I didn't even have to think about that. "What can you tell me about Armstrong Industries?"

He gazed at the sky and gave that a bit of thought. Finally, he said "Not a whole lot. Folks around here were worried when Armstrong first showed up, myself included. You know, bombs and all. The biggest concern was that there'd be an accident. I'm happy to say that hasn't happened yet. And they keep a low profile, if you know what I mean. They're quiet. Good citizens. Good neighbors."

That was good to know. "I've seen some of them at the Hog Jaw Diner a couple of times."

Snow shrugged. "What can I say? Everybody's gotta eat somewhere."

It was time to change the subject. "What about that motorcycle club that comes here weekends? What's their name?" I asked.

"You mean the Brave Hearts?" He rolled his eyes. "To tell you the truth, I don't really know much about them. For the most part, they seem to be nothing more than a bunch of middle-aged guys cutting loose on the weekends."

Hmmm. "For the most part?" I echoed. "Have they ever caused any kind of problem?"

"Only once. And in the end it didn't amount to much."

"What happened?"

"That old Indian fellow from down by Pinson filed a complaint, saying the Brave Hearts were trespassing on his land."

"Do you mean the area near the top of Hog Jaw Mountain?"

"I mean the whole darn mountain, and the woods around it. The shaman said those folks were causing irreparable damage to his sacred mound."

"And were they?"

"They were riding around the area, up and down Hog Jaw Road. And hiking in the surrounding woods as well. But there was nothing much I could do about it. It's public land, the road and the mountain, at least most of it. Technically, the tribe only owns the mound at the top, although they'd probably tell you otherwise."

I thought back to what Shaman Wakham had told me. The issue was a tricky one.

"How did you resolve the problem?"

"I spoke with the Brave Hearts. Explained the medicine man's point of view. Asked them to be a little more respectful of the land—as a good-will gesture."

"Did that work?" I asked.

"Has so far."

"So the Brave Hearts are behaving themselves better?"

"Either that or that old Indian has just given up complaining about it."

Based on my conversation with the shaman, I doubted that. "Tell me, Sheriff, who owns Hog Jaw Road?"

Snow shrugged. "The county, as far as I know."

Hmmm. "The county certainly maintains it in beautiful condition, particularly for an unpaved road, don't you think?"

"If you say so. I never really noticed."

"Does the road get much use?"

"I wouldn't think so. I don't get up there much myself. We don't patrol there very often. There's no real reason to. From what I can see, that road is nothing more than a quicker way to get from nowhere on one side of the mountain to nowhere on the other side, with nothing but a small parking lot along the way. There's no point wasting time patrolling there." He paused and chewed on his bottom lip. "Come to think of it, there's no point putting money into maintaining the road either, is there?"

And yet maintain it they did. The question was why.

Before I could give that much thought, Officer Graham emerged from room 8. "All done in there," he announced. "Shouldn't take but a few minutes to get that set of prints you want. You said that lady was in the motel office, right?"

Graham and Snow started walking toward the motel office. I was about to join them when my phone rang.

Chapter 18

Late Friday morning

I grabbed my phone quickly before it went into voice mail. I was in no mood to play telephone tag today, even with somebody identified as Caller Unknown. "Hello?" I said as I watched Snow and Graham walk away.

"Hi. I'm looking for Amy Lynch," a woman said. "She left me a message a while ago." The drawl in her voice suggested that she was a local.

"This is Amy."

"My name is Olivia Franklin. I'm guessing you're that insurance lady Chuckie told me would be calling. He said there was something you wanted to ask me."

Chuckie? "Yes. I understand you were at the Hog Jaw Motel the night of the shooting. I'm hoping you can tell me what you saw or heard."

That was met with a few moments of dead silence.

Finally, Olivia said, "I don't know how much help I can be, but I'm happy to tell you what I can. I can't really chat with you now, though. I'm on my coffee break. I get off work at 1:00. Any chance we could we do it then?"

I didn't want to interview the woman over the phone anyway. Face-to-face meetings always had a way of conveying so much more information. Body language could be a wonderful thing. "That would be great," I told her. "Is there someplace convenient where we can meet?"

"There's a diner next door to the motel where I work. That'd be good. We can grab some lunch while we talk."

That sounded good to me. Lunch was always a plus. "Where do you work?" I asked.

"The Snuggle Inn in Davisville. It's not too far out of Hog Jaw."

"Actually, I know exactly where it is. I'll meet you there at 1:00."

"Okay. How will I know you?"

"I'll be driving a red Mustang convertible. Top down," I told her, grateful that Pete hadn't taken it with him to Hog Jaw Road.

She laughed. "You and Chuckie and your Mustangs. I'll never understand what it is about those cars that people love so much. Oh well, whatever. See you later."

Later came after a pleasant drive through the countryside. I was hungry by the time I pulled into the Davisville Diner's parking lot a few minutes before 1:00. There were at least a dozen vehicles there, most of them older model pickups. Either the food was pretty good there, or it was the only place around. I'd find out shortly.

A youngish woman dressed in a chambermaid uniform and soiled sneakers walked toward my car. She was tall and thin with bleached blonde hair seriously in need of a touch-up. The badge on her uniform identified her as Olivia.

We exchanged greetings and went into the diner, securing what appeared to be the last available table. A young girl with braces on her teeth and an unfortunate complexion arrived with pen and pad in hand. "Good afternoon, folks, I'm Martine," she said. "What can I get for y'all today?"

I decided to forego my favorite lunch - a double bacon cheeseburger and a side of onion rings. I had been overdoing the hot grease lately.

Feeling smug about my healthy decision, I ordered a Caesar salad instead, with chicken. I would have liked it with shrimp, but West Tennessee was a long way from the ocean. Sometimes it pays to play it safe.

"I'll have the usual," Olivia told her. "I eat here a lot," she said to me.

Once Martine was off to order our food, I pulled my phone out of my purse. "Do you mind if I record this?" I asked Olivia. I hoped the background noise in the diner wouldn't interfere too much.

She shook her head. "I suppose it's all right. As long as you keep what I tell you confidential, that is. I can't afford to have everybody in West Tennessee knowing my personal business, if you know what I mean."

I assumed that she was referring to her relationship with Chuck Andrews. "Not to worry," I assured her. "I'll be as discreet as possible."

Olivia let out a noisy sigh of relief. "So what can I tell you?"

"For the record, please confirm that you were at the Hog Jaw Motel the night of the recent shootings."

She nodded.

"The phone recorder can't hear your nod," I told her.

"Yeah, right," she said, blushing slightly. "I'm not used to being recorded you know. Yes, I was there that night."

"What room were you in?"

"Room 1."

I called up a mental picture of the motel. Rooms 1and 2 were on the far side of the office, closer to the woods than to the diner and the garage. Also about as far as a body could get from the scene of the shootings. "Was anybody else there with you?"

Olivia looked at me like I had two heads and a tail. "Well, yeah. Chuckie was there. I thought you already knew that."

"I do," I said. "This is just for the record."

"Room 1 is kind of our special place," Olivia continued. "Lillie keeps it open for us, as much as she can."

Customer service at its finest, particularly when your regular guests have naughty secrets to protect.

Martine chose that moment to deliver our food. Olivia attacked her Italian sub and chips like she hadn't eaten in days. I picked at my salad, concentrating on the chicken. A couple minutes later, I resumed my interview. "Please tell me everything you remember about what happened that night."

She closed her eyes for a moment, then opened them with a frown. "Well, let's see. I fell asleep early that night. Chuckie and I had been drinking red wine. It always makes me sleepy. A loud noise woke me up out of a deep sleep."

"What kind of a noise?" I deliberately avoided mentioning anything about a gunshot. No point in leading the witness.

"It was a Harley. With some idiot revving the engine. It pissed me off royally. I had been having such a nice dream. Anyway, I went to the window to see who it was, so I could give whoever it was hell the next time I saw him."

"You know the bikers?" I asked. *Interesting.*

"Most of them. They're at the motel a lot. So am I."

I searched my memory banks for the names of the two bikers. "And who was it?" I asked, expecting her to say either Buster Dolan or Gary Miller.

"It was a guy named Snake."

I shuddered. "Please tell me that isn't his real name."

She shrugged. "I can't say for sure. That's what everybody calls him. I think it's because the scar on his cheek looks like a snake. They all go by crazy nicknames. If you ask me, I think that's sort of stupid. Like they never got over being kids, you know?"

"Do you know Snake well?"

"Not really," she answered, apparently choosing not to elaborate, let alone volunteer anything. It seemed I'd need to dig for details.

"But well enough to know his name," I prodded.

"Yeah, right. Mostly because that's what I've always heard Lillie call him."

"Do you see this Snake fellow at the motel often?"

"I suppose so. He's there kind of a lot." *And apparently so was Olivia.*

Still, that was a surprise. "It's my understanding that the bikers are there mostly on weekends," I said.

Olivia nodded. "That's true. Except for Snake. I see him during the week as well, mostly on Thursdays."

That struck me as a wee bit peculiar. "Are you sure about the day being Thursday?"

"Absolutely." She stared down at her hands. "You see, Thursday is bowling league night around here. So that's when Chuckie and I usually, you know, get together. Because his wife thinks he's bowling."

I couldn't help but ask, "Does Snake go bowling as well?"

Olivia shook her head.

"Any idea what Snake was doing at the motel that night?"

Olivia bit her lower lip. "I shouldn't really be telling you this. I mean, after all, it is none of my business, but …"

"But what?"

"He talks to Lillie a lot. A whole lot. Sometimes in the parking lot. Sometimes he goes over to the office. Sometimes they take a walk in the woods."

I was beginning to see a whole new and interesting side to Lillie. I tucked that nugget of info away to examine later. In the meantime, I said, "Please tell me everything you can remember about that night."

Olivia nodded. "So, like I was saying, the noise from Snake's motorcycle woke me up, and annoyed me no end. I threw on some clothes so I could go out and give him a piece of my mind. And that's when I noticed that Chuckie wasn't in the room. Guess I must have been sleeping pretty soundly not to hear him leave. I opened the door and spotted him way down the other end of the motel with his arms around Lillie, patting her on the back like he was trying to comfort her or something."

She paused and took a long, deep breath.

"Then what did you do?" I prodded.

"I was just about to go over to see what was up with Chuckie and Lillie when Snake stopped me. He told me I should run to my car and get out of Dodge as fast as I could, so I wouldn't have to get involved in whatever it was that was happening. Just then, I saw the cops drive up and decided Snake was probably right. Better to stay out of things. Sure didn't want my name in the local paper saying that I was there with Chuckie. I mean, his wife actually reads the newspaper every day."

I closed my eyes for a moment trying to visualize the scene. Then something occurred to me. "How did you get out of the parking lot without anybody stopping you? The sheriff told me he asked all the motel guests to stick around to be interviewed."

"My car wasn't in the lot," she responded. "I had it parked out behind my room. That's what I usually do. There's a spot there that's just big enough for my Civic. And it's out of the way, so almost nobody knows that I'm there."

"Almost nobody?" I asked.

"Yeah. Lillie knows. It was actually her idea. She's good like that, trying to protect our privacy. After all, we are regular guests."

"And how did you get down the road without being noticed?"

"I drove around the far side of the diner and parked behind the garage until I was sure the coast was clear. Snake was there too, on his Harley. I was surprised he had been able to get it there without the sheriff noticing him."

"Did you and Snake speak at that point?"

"Nope." Olivia looked at her watch. "Listen, I'm happy to help you here, but it's getting near two thirty. I've got a three o'clock mani-pedi scheduled, and it's at least a twenty-minute drive. How about we pay up fast so I can get on my way?"

"I'll take care of the bill," I told her. "And thanks so much for your help. If I have any further questions, I'll let you know."

"Thanks," she said as she dashed out the door.

I watched her leave, then gathered up my things. Later on, I'd take a good long listen to everything she had told me. There had to be something there that would help my case.

Chapter 19

Friday afternoon

It was nearly three o'clock by the time I got back to the Hog Jaw Motel. I expected that Pete would be back from his morning hike by now. He wasn't. That worried me. What in the world could he be doing on Hog Jaw Mountain all this time? I texted him to confirm that he was all right, hoping that there was cell service up there. Happily, he answered me right away, saying he was fine and enjoying the day. No mention of when he thought he might be back. I tried my best not to let that annoy me.

It was slightly out-of-character for Pete to spend so much time in the great outdoors. On the other hand, it was also a relief. It afforded me some time to review my conversation with Olivia and update my notes online. Once that was done, I planned to check in with Peggy and ask her to take a look at the notes. Maybe she'd notice something that I missed. She was usually pretty good at that.

I was nearly done reviewing my notes when something popped into my mind—something I should have realized earlier. Up until now, I had accepted Sheriff Snow's version of who was at the motel that night. From what Olivia had told me, I now knew there were at least two more people at the motel that night that Snow may not have been aware of.

These folks hadn't been interviewed. I needed to know who else may have been there and if, or why, Snow didn't know about them.

I saved my updated notes and shut down the laptop. It was time to have a serious discussion with Lillie. I locked the room and headed out.

I ran into Noreen in the parking lot, or, rather, she ran into me. She was driving out of the lot and came close to mowing me down. She stopped just in time, then rolled down her window.

"I'm glad I ran into you," she said.

Poor choice of words. "What's up?"

She gave me what she probably thought was a pleasant smile. She was wrong. "I'm wondering where things stand on Jake's life insurance payment," she said. "Shouldn't Lillie be receiving a check soon? Is there a problem?"

I chose not to answer that question. Instead, I told her, "It has only been a little over a week since Jake passed away. Payments usually take from 30 to 60 days to be issued, even under the best of circumstances. I'm waiting for additional information from the authorities to determine exactly what happened the night Jake died."

Noreen scowled. "And how long is *that* going to take?" She revved her engine and took off in a huff. Apparently she didn't expect a response.

With Noreen gone, Lillie was alone in the office. That was a good thing for me. I had a feeling that she'd be more forthcoming with me without Noreen hovering over her. I found the new widow staring at her computer screen as if it might possibly provide the details of the meaning of life. She looked up and smiled when she heard the door. At least somebody seemed pleased to see me.

"Hello, Amy," she said, swiveling around in her chair to face me at the front desk. "How are you today? Do you have any news for me? How is your investigation going?"

I leaned on the counter, looking down at her—an obvious attempt to achieve a position of power. Those of us under five feet tall often do things like that. "Everything is moving right along," I told her. "I hope to have it all wrapped up soon."

"That would be great," she said. "Is there anything I can do to help?"

"That's actually what brought me in here," I told her. "I have a question about the night of the shooting."

"Ask away." She raised her hands, palms open, as if in surrender.

"Could I please take a look at your guest register for the night in question? I need to confirm a few things, for the record."

She hesitated for a few seconds, then rose to stand at the counter. She turned the register book around so I could see it. I loved the fact that she kept hand-written records. They were trickier to alter than the computerized version. I studied the page in question. And found no mention of Olivia Franklin or Chuck Andrews or the biker called Snake. Was that an oversight or was it deliberate? And did it matter to my case?

Lillie gave me a deer-in-the headlights look. "Is there a problem?"

"I'm not sure," I said.

"What do you mean?"

"I had a conversation with Olivia Franklin today. She admitted she was here that night, with Chuck. She told me that a biker named Snake was here as well. She said they both were able to slip away unnoticed. What can you tell me about that?"

Lillie nearly choked. She dropped the motel register from her hands and turned a sorry shade of red. "Well, uh," she stammered, "you see … I mean, the thing is …"

I stood silently before her, giving her a chance to compose herself.

She dropped into her chair and looked up at me. "Olivia was right. She was here."

"Then why isn't she listed in the register?" I asked. "I don't see a listing here for Chuck either. How did that happen?"

"I didn't exactly check them in, if you know what I mean."

I wasn't sure I did know. "Why not?"

"To keep things quiet," she said, wiping a tear from her eye.

"What kind of things?" I knew the answer to this, but wanted to see what Lillie would have to say.

"Well, you see, she and Chuck are both friends of mine. And I do them favors when they need them, and when I can."

"Favors like letting them stay here for free and keeping it off the records?"

She shook her head. "No. No. They pay me. I just don't put them on the records. To give them some privacy."

"Privacy? What do you mean?" *As if I didn't know.*

"Well, you see," she stammered, "it's like this. Olivia and I go way back. We've been best friends forever. She and Chuck are in love. They have been for ages. But Chuck's wife won't let him go. She threatened to keep the kids away from him if he left her. And he couldn't live with that. He loves those kids something fierce. So I give the two of them a place where they can be together without the whole world knowing about it."

All in the name of true love! Oh well, none of my business. "What do you do with the money they pay you? Is that off the books as well?"

She nodded. "I set it aside. In case of emergencies. You know, sort of like having a Swiss bank account."

I couldn't help but wonder what she actually planned to do with the money. "And what about the fellow known as Snake? I don't see that name listed here either. Nor any other name showing a guest in room 2. Do you have the same sort of arrangement with him?"

"I do," she replied. The guilt in her voice was almost palpable. "It's like with Olivia and Chuck. Snake is a good friend too."

I couldn't help but wonder how good. "Do you know Snake's real name?"

"Sorry. I don't."

And yet she let him stay at the motel without registering. What was up with that? "Do you know where Snake lives?"

"West of here. Somewhere on the other side of Trenton."

"And he's one of the Brave Hearts?"

She nodded.

I had one final question. "I thought the Brave Hearts were only here on weekends. Do you have any idea why Snake was here on a Thursday?"

She had no answer for that.

I didn't press the point. Thanking her for her time, I returned to my room.

Still no Pete.

I gathered my thoughts then placed a call to Peggy.

"Hello to you," she greeted me. "How are things in the back of beyond?"

"Getting more interesting all the time," I said. I gave her a brief but thorough overview of what I had learned today. "As you can tell, there are now a few more characters for you and Tiffany to check out."

"Not a problem. But tell me, what do you think is up with Lillie and her secret slush fund? Was she saving up to be able to leave Jake?"

"Good question. No answer. At least not yet."

"But if that's what she was up to, wouldn't that also show either a motive or at least a proclivity to want to be rid of Jake?"

I had no answer for that either. And I wasn't quite ready to deal with proclivities at the moment. "I suppose anything is possible," I said. "In the meantime, what's happening in Boston? Anything I need, or want, to know about?"

Peggy let out a heavy sigh. "The biggest news around here today is Tiffany. And none of it is good."

"What's up?"

Peggy took in a big noisy breath. "There's no easy way to say this. She's about ready to quit." Her voice choked. "She just can't take it anymore from George."

Actually, neither could I, but at least I had ways to avoid the man most of the time. "What happened?"

"Her car broke down the other day. It's in the garage waiting for a part to come in. So Tiff has to take the bus to work. And she has been late twice this week."

"How late?" I asked.

"Fifteen minutes or so. Truly no big deal. But that nasty so-and-so George is being totally unreasonable. He threatened to put her on report if it happened again. Or to dock her pay. Can you believe that?"

I realized how angry Peggy was. Calling someone a "so-and-so" was the closest she came to an actual insult.

"Tiffany explained to him exactly what happened," Peggy continued. "And he said she better take an earlier bus if she wants to keep her job. And he better not catch her taking long lunches or too many coffee breaks. Next thing you know he'll be timing her bathroom breaks as well, if you can imagine that."

Actually I could, knowing George as I did. But I kept that to myself—for the moment anyhow. "Don't worry about George," I told her. "I'll deal with him soon enough. And don't stress out about the workload in the meantime. Just do what you can for now. We'll work it out when I get back. I'll go to Mark about it if I have to."

"Sounds good to me," Peggy said. "I'll be fine. I just hope Tiffany doesn't up and quit before you do get back."

"Tell her to hang in there. I'll be home soon enough." At least I hoped I would.

Chapter 20

Late Friday afternoon

Pete was in the room when I returned, sitting barefoot on the bed examining his feet. "Oh, there you are," he greeted me. "I'm thinking I need to get some thicker socks. There's one heck of a bad blister on my heel. It's a good thing I remembered to pack some Band-Aids."

Odd, but good. I wondered if perhaps he was a bit out of shape in general and not getting as much exercise as he needed, but decided to keep that thought to myself. Instead, I asked, "How was your day?"

"Not at all what I expected," he replied.

Now that was interesting. "How so?" *Perhaps it might help my case?*

"I'll tell you all about it over dinner," he said. "Speaking of which, can we please eat soon? I'm absolutely starving."

"Sure, why not?" I said. My own lunch had definitely been less than satisfying. "Why are you so hungry? I thought you brought food with you. Wasn't it enough?"

"I did. And it should have been enough. But I ate it all way earlier than I had planned to. I don't know why I was so hungry."

Maybe because you took off in a rush this morning and didn't fin-ish your breakfast? I decided not to voice this thought. I also scolded my-self for being so cranky and nit-picky with Pete. What was up with that? The last thing I knew, I was in love with the guy.

I checked my watch. It was just before 5:00. "Are you okay to eat at the diner again?" I asked him.

He let out something between a laugh and a sigh. "I suppose. At least it's convenient, and the food is pretty good. But do you think we might try to find someplace, anyplace, else in the area sometime soon? Just for a change?"

"Of course we can," I told him. "But let's not forget, it is important to my case to keep an eye on the locals."

Pete gazed up at the ceiling. "And, as usual, the case must come first. Okay. Ames, I get that. I really do. That's why we're here. But please tell me we can broaden our horizons in some small way over the weekend and maybe find another dining option. Please tell me that you're planning to take some time off over the weekend as well. You know, 'all work and no play', and all that."

He was right. A night out, fine dining included, would do us both some good. We'd think of something.

"Good plan." I gestured toward the door. "In the meantime, shall we head over to the diner so we can beat the local dinner rush?"

And off we went.

We were the first customers to arrive at the Hog Jaw Diner. As usual, the aroma of fresh-baked bread met us at the door, as well as the scent of hot grease. Oddly enough, even that was appealing to me. I was hungrier than I thought.

Walt greeted us like we were old friends. Minnie gave us her usual scowl, then suggested we sample her famous fried chicken. We decided to give it a try, even though it wasn't the infamous local gas station variety. Walt brought us our usual beer and wine and we settled in to the now-familiar setting. Little by little, a few other customers began to trickle in, the usual variety of bleary-eyed truckers and clean-cut fellows wearing shirts sporting the Armstrong Industries logo. Nothing of any particular interest, just another night in the Hog Jaw Diner.

I sipped my wine and said to Pete, "Now tell me about your day. You were gone a lot longer than I thought you'd be. I'm assuming that's a good sign. What was so unexpected?"

Pete put down his beer and leaned forward, elbows on the table. "Mostly just the number of people I encountered."

"How so? I thought the area had a regular hiking trail. Open to the public."

"That's true." He closed his eyes as if seeing the trail again in his head. "But today is Friday, a working day for most people. It's also a school day. I had sort of expected that I'd have the place mostly to myself. My plan was to hike to the top of the mountain, find a cozy spot to sit, on a rock or something, read my book and enjoy some solitude, maybe do a little day-dreaming. Yet there they were, all of them, out enjoying the beauties of nature, mostly in pairs or small groups."

I put my wine glass down on the table and waited, wondering if there was a punch line coming. When there wasn't, I asked, "And exactly who were these people?"

"Kids, teenage boys mostly, drinking beer and smoking cigarettes. Based on the number of them, the schools must have been half empty. I can sort of relate to that. After all, I was a teenage boy once myself. There were also some young lovers, apparently in search of a place to be alone— and not having much luck from what I could see."

He stared off into space. "Then there were the hikers."

Our meals arrived. We fell silent for a bit while we sampled our chicken. It was better than good. And definitely better than the gas station variety I had sampled the other day. I promised myself I'd go easy on the French fries, though, to leave room for dessert. Finally, I said to Pete,

"Nothing that you've told me comes as much of a surprise. I imagine the mountain is a wonderful place to hike in such beautiful spring weather."

"Agreed," he replied, "but like I said, we're talking about a Friday morning in the spring. And some of these hikers struck me as a little bit odd."

"How so?"

He gave this some thought. "They seemed to come in two varieties. Some of them appeared to be seasoned hikers. You know the type - worn jeans, faded baseball caps, dirty old hiking boots, well-used knapsacks bursting at the seams. Others seemed to be the newbies. Some of them wore khakis. Others had spotless jeans that looked like they had just been pressed. Also mostly hoodies. And sneakers, really clean sneakers. They just didn't seem to fit in."

"I get the picture," I said. "Did these 'newbies' have knapsacks too?"

"They did. They looked brand new too. Not at all well-used." He took a long slow drink of his beer, then said, "The thing that struck me the most was that they all seemed to know each other. The seasoned pros and the newbies alike. They nodded to each other when they passed on the trail. Exchanged greetings. I saw a couple of them engrossed in conversations as well - more than once."

"Hmmm. Maybe they all see each other often on the trail. Or perhaps people are just friendlier to strangers in Tennessee than they are in Boston."

"Anything's possible," he responded. "But that's not all. I began walking to the other side of the mountain hoping to find a quiet place to read. But that simply wasn't meant to be. That was when I ran into the shaman. You know, the one from Pinson."

I dropped my fork onto my plate, trying to picture that. "The old guy? What was his name? Joseph something or other. Are you telling me he was hiking in the woods?"

"No, not him," Pete replied. "It was the younger guy, Thomas. He's Joseph's grandson. The shaman-in-training."

I recalled our conversation with the two of them at the mounds in Pinson. "That's right. Joseph told us it was his responsibility to maintain the mound in Hog Jaw."

Pete nodded. "That job has fallen to the grandson now. Joseph told me that the local indigenous people consider the entire mountain a sacred place. And apparently things aren't going so well for Thomas lately."

"What's the problem?" I asked as I sipped some wine. "If I remember correctly, Joseph said something about the area becoming run-down over the past few years. And that he was working to restore it. He didn't tell us exactly why the place is sacred."

"Thomas told me," Pete said.

"And?"

"It's where they grow their mushrooms."

"Mushrooms?" I exclaimed just loudly enough that the people at a nearby table turned our way. "Did he tell you why?" I had a feeling I knew the answer, but wanted to hear what the shaman had told Pete.

"It has something to do with their ceremonies. It seems these people are still heavily into practicing the 'old ways.'" He finger-quoted the last two words.

I thought back to what I had learned in college. "I'm guessing what they're growing are not your everyday garden-variety mushrooms."

"You are guessing correctly." He finished the last of his beer, then added, "They're what is often referred to as magic mushrooms."

"I believe their official name is psilocybin," I told him.

"Is it legal to grow them?" Pete asked.

I did a quick google search on my phone. "Only in a few states. And from what I'm reading here, Tennessee isn't one of them."

"So the shamans are engaged in illegal activity," Pete said.

I sighed as the ever-present lawyer side of Pete reared its occasionally ugly head. "I suppose you could look at it that way. Or you could view it as the Native Americans from whom the Europeans stole this land are still struggling to retain their identity and beliefs. I find that something worth fighting for."

"And there you go again," Pete said, "always the champion of the underdog."

Not interested in arguing, I let that slide. "What else did the young shaman tell you?"

"He offered to show me the mushroom patch, or whatever you call it."

"That's pretty cool. What was it like?"

Pete shook his head. "We were just about to head there when a couple of hikers came by. They didn't say anything, just stood there giving us nasty looks. I got the impression Thomas knew them."

"How were they dressed?" I asked him by way of interruption.

"Dressed? Does it matter?" He shrugged.

"It might," I told him. "Were they wearing jeans or khakis?"

"I don't remember," Pete said. "Sorry. Anyway, as soon as they left, Thomas said he needed to get going and suggested we visit the area tomorrow morning. I'm going to meet him there around 10:00."

"Did he say anything else? Like why he had to leave so suddenly? Or who the hikers were?" I asked.

Pete shook his head. "He didn't get a chance. My phone rang at that point. It was Moira. I had to speak with her."

"Is everything all right at the office?"

"Yes and no. There is an issue that needs to be addressed, but it's nothing I can't handle from here. I'll do a little research then get back to her tomorrow."

"I'm a little surprised that you had decent cell coverage on the top of the mountain in the back of beyond," I said.

"It surprised me as well. I imagine there must be a cell tower somewhere nearby. What's surprising is that there would be much of a demand for cell service this far from more heavily populated areas."

"I suppose." Then something occurred to me. "Didn't Shaman Joseph tell us somebody wanted to buy that land?"

Pete nodded. "He did. I'm beginning to wonder not only who, but also why. Really, what plans could anybody have that would involve owning the top of that mountain? It's not like you could build much of anything up there."

Walt stopped by our table to clear away our dinner plates. "Are you folks interested in some dessert? Apple pie's hot out of the oven."

Neither of us could resist such an offer.

We lingered over pie and coffee. I filled Pete in on my day. For a change, it had been less interesting than his. We headed back to the room. Pete needed to do some online research for Moira. Sad to say, I was happy that would keep him busy for a while. I had work to do.

I was updating my case notes when the roar of multiple motorcycles erupted in the parking lot. The bikers had arrived for the weekend. I checked back in my notes for the names of those I needed to speak with—hopefully Gary Miller, and/or the ever-popular Snake. Tomorrow could turn out to be interesting.

Chapter 21

Saturday morning

Everybody was up early the next morning. The bikers saw to that. From what I couldn't help but hear, they met in the parking lot and headed over to the diner en masse.

I jumped out of bed and dressed quickly. My plan was to go to the diner and speak with as many of them as possible before they took off for the open road. They must have gulped down their breakfasts at break-neck speed though. I saw several of them leaving the diner before I even got to the front door. I guessed they may have ordered their food to go.

It was time for Plan B: hang out in the parking lot and make nice with them, hoping they'd take the time to answer a few questions before taking off for parts unknown. Foiled again. They were pleasant enough responding to my cheery good mornings, but had no interest in small talk. Most of them smiled in my direction; a few of them wished me a nice day; then they mounted their motorcycles and dashed away with a loud roar.

When the noxious scent from the exhaust cleared from the parking lot, one lone cycle remained. I scanned the area for a straggler. Nobody in sight. Then I noticed a fellow outside of a room on the other side of the motel office. His leather jacket and boots screamed biker. He was speaking with Lillie. They were standing close together, their eyes fixed on each other. What was up with that?

They finally spotted me. Lillie gave me a shy little wave and scurried into the office. I got a good look at the biker as he headed my way. The scar on his cheek suggested he might be Snake. He smiled and said, "Good morning, ma'am. How're you doing today?"

I gazed up at the sky and said a quick thank-you to the universe for arranging this encounter for me. There was one biker I really wanted to chat with—and here he was. It was almost enough to make me believe in coincidence. Almost, but not quite.

I pasted on a smile and walked his way. "I'm doing just fine, thanks," I said. "Looks like it's going to be a beautiful day."

"That's for darn sure."

"You better hurry if you're going to catch up with the rest of the guys," I told him. "They sure seemed in a big rush to be anywhere but here."

"You've got that right," he said. "It seems there's no point wasting time on a day like this." He made no move toward his bike as he said this.

"Aren't you joining them?" I asked.

He shook his head. "Not this morning. I've got some business to take care of first. Riding is just a hobby with me. Making a living needs to come first. I know where those guys are headed. I'll catch up with them later." He walked over to my rented Mustang and gave it a long, loving look. "Nice looking ride. Is it yours?"

"No. It's a rental. I've got one back home, though. Brand new. Bright red. Convertible. What more could you ask for?"

"V6 or V8?" he asked.

"The one at home is a V8. I'm not sure about this one."

"Mind if I check under the hood?"

"Be my guest." *And please, take your time about it so you and I can have a nice long chat.*

He walked to the driver's door, paused a moment looking at the handle, then looked over at me expectantly.

"Oops," I said as I grabbed my key and beeped it to unlock the car.

The biker reached into the car and released the hood latch under the dashboard. Then he walked to the front of the car, popped the hood and poked his head inside. "V6," he said with a sad shake of his head as he lowered the hood. "A shame in such an otherwise beautiful machine. By the way, how do you do. Folks call me Snake."

"It's nice to meet you, Snake," I said, reaching in my pocket for my card. "I was actually hoping I'd run into you here."

That earned me a wide-eyed look.

I handed him the card and said, "I'm from New England Casualty and Indemnity. Here to investigate Jake Taylor's death."

His eyes got even wider. "Insurance, huh? It's good to know Jake had some. I'm sure Lillie could use the money right about now. But what is there to investigate? I mean, really, a man dies and the insurance company writes a check, right?"

"It's not always that simple," I told him. "Particularly when the policy is less than a year old."

Snake started to respond to that. I cut him off, hoping to avoid a boring discussion about any of the possible issues that could crop up with a life insurance claim. "I understand that you were here at the motel the night of the shooting. I'm hoping that you can answer a few questions for me."

"Who told you I was here?" he grumbled. "Lillie?"

I shook my head. "Lillie didn't mention you. Olivia Franklin did."

"Oh yeah, right. She and Chuck were in the room next to mine." He paused and looked everywhere but at me. "I really can't tell you very much. Once the commotion started, I got out of the way as fast as I could."

"Why was that?"

He hesitated, then finally replied, "Well, you see, the sheriff was already here, so I figured things were under control. And Chuck was with Lillie, so I didn't worry about her. And … and I really wanted to avoid Jake."

The obvious question was why Snake didn't want to see Jake. I left that unasked for the moment, waiting to see where Snake would go with it.

"You see," he began, "it's like this. A week or so ago, Jake and I had a slight disagreement. About some damage he thought I had caused to a room. But I hadn't. And I wasn't in the mood for a fight that night. So I just took off."

Did that mean he didn't know Jake was dead at that point? That made more sense to me than wondering if Snake had killed Jake over a disagreement.

I put that thought on hold for a moment and started at the beginning. "My understanding is that the Brave Heart bikers are here mostly on the weekends."

Snake nodded.

"The shooting was on a Thursday night. I'm wondering what brought you here in the middle of the week."

That comment earned me a non-committal shrug. "Business. When I'm working out this way, Hog Jaw is a convenient place to spend the night. It has sort of become my home away from home."

"So you stay here often?"

"Any time my business brings me out this way."

"What is it that you do?"

"I'm in sales."

"What do you sell?"

"Pharmaceuticals."

Before I could ask Snake anything more, Pete emerged from our motel room. "There you are, Ames," he said as he gave Snake the once-over. "I was afraid you might have gone to breakfast without me."

Snake answered for me. "Actually I've been taking up this lovely lady's time checking out her Mustang. One of the coolest cars ever made, if you ask me. Well, guess I better be going now." He jumped on his motorcycle and roared off before I could even introduce Pete to him.

I smiled at Pete. "That was Snake. I'll tell you about him at breakfast." We made our way to the diner.

It was quiet there, just a few truckers who had probably overslept. Our food arrived quickly. As we ate, we compared plans for the day. Pete's sounded like more fun than mine. I'd be doing my best to wrap up my investigation so I could head back to Boston while I still had a job. Pete was going to Hog Jaw Mountain to meet Shaman Thomas and see the mound where Thomas grew the illegal magic mushrooms.

We were just leaving the diner when a fellow approached us in the parking lot. He wore grease-stained overalls, an Atlanta Braves baseball cap and a black armband to signify his mourning. He reeked of petroleum products. I guessed it was Jake's brother Ike. "Morning, Ms. Lynch," he said. "Things are quiet for me at the moment. If you're not too busy, this would be a good time for us to chat."

Pete checked his watch. "And I better be going if I'm going to be on time meeting Thomas. I'll see you sometime this afternoon."

Sometime this afternoon? That was a bit vague, particularly for Pete. He usually planned things in minute detail. What was up with him all of a sudden?

He was gone before I could react. Oh well, I'd catch up with him later. For the moment, I followed Ike over to the Hog Jaw Garage.

Chapter 22

Later Saturday morning

The garage and convenience store were both quiet at the moment. I hoped they would stay that way, but if they didn't, I could roll with it somehow.

Ike surveyed his little kingdom, such as it was. "Hope you don't mind chatting out front here," he began. "I've got to watch things. My wife usually takes care of the store. She isn't feeling well today, so I'm doing double duty. We can't afford to lose business you know."

"Not a problem," I assured him. "Are you usually busy here?"

He nodded. "Busy and then some these days. Things have picked up quite a bit since Armstrong moved in. I can't complain about that."

"Is it busier at the motel as well?"

"Everywhere," he told me. "The garage, the store, the motel, the diner, all of it. And now there'll be one less of us to handle it all."

That was my cue to get down to business. "I'm sorry about your brother. This must be very difficult for you."

"Thanks. I've got to tell you, there's nothing easy about any of it." His eyes teared up. "And I've got to ask you something that everybody's wondering about."

"What's that?"

"Since when is life insurance so complicated? Why can't you folks just write a check, then go back to where you come from and leave us alone?"

"I wish it were that simple," I told him. "Things get complicated when firearms are involved. Or when policies are less than a year old."

"What do you mean by that?" he growled. "Are you saying that you folks think somebody's trying to cheat you?"

"No," I answered. "Not at all. It's just standard insurance policy procedure. I know it's uncomfortable for people, but I have no choice. I didn't make the rules. I do have to follow them, though, if I want my paycheck."

"So the sooner you and I have our chat, the sooner you'll be finished here?" Ike asked. "And gone?"

"That is the plan." I pulled out my cell phone. "Is it all right with you if I record this? It's a lot easier than trying to take notes."

He shrugged. "Whatever works for you. I don't know what I can do to help you anyway. I wasn't anywhere near the motel that night, you know. I live nearly five miles away."

"When did you hear about the incident?"

"Not until the next day. Sheriff Stone notified us all in the morning, when we came to open up the garage and the diner."

"Did you hear much talk about what happened? What were people saying?"

"Nothing much," he told me. "Just the usual gossip and rumors. Hardly worth repeating."

I thought perhaps I should be the judge of that. For the moment, I simply said, "Actually, I was hoping you could give me a little background information."

Ike raised his eyebrows. "Background on what?"

"Hog Jaw in general," I told him. "And anything you can tell me about the people involved in the recent tragedy."

He shuffled his feet and stared off toward the motel. "I'll tell you what I can. But it ain't much. What do you want to know?"

I did a quick search of my mental checklist. "For starters, did Jake have any enemies that you were aware of?"

Ike let out a sound halfway between a snort and a guffaw. "Jake? No way. Hell, everybody liked the guy. He was a good man. People knew that. They respected him for it."

"Did he have a lot of friends?" I asked.

"Not so's you'd notice," Ike said. "I mean, he was friendly enough with folks. But he was quiet too. Kept to himself a lot. And didn't take any nonsense from anybody. Ever."

Yet everybody liked him. Hmmm. "Are you saying that he didn't socialize much?"

Ike nodded. "Right. Can't say that he did. He was usually too busy at the motel most of the time. The only time Jake ever really got out was on bowling night."

I remembered what Olivia had told me. "Bowling night is Thursday, isn't it?"

"Yeah, it is. But Jake didn't go last week. He had sprained his wrist fixing something or other. Needed to give it a rest."

"What about with Lillie? Did she and Jake do much socializing as a couple?"

That earned an outright guffaw from Ike. "Lillie? Are you kidding? No way."

"Why not?"

"Mostly because nobody liked the woman. Never did."

Now that was interesting. "How come?"

"She was too stuck-up. That's how come. She was a cute little thing in high school. All the boys were after her. That's not a good way to make girlfriends, if you know what I mean."

I knew what he meant. "But that was a long time ago," I reminded him.

"It seems like some girls don't forget these things. And Lillie never really got over it either. Once a flirt, always a flirt. She sure loved the boys' attention."

"How did Jake feel about that?"

"I can't rightly say. He didn't talk much about that sort of thing. Didn't like to get too personal, even with me."

"How does Lillie get along with your parents? Are they close?"

"Not so you'd notice. I mean, they don't fight or anything. More like they all retreat to neutral corners and do their own things."

"What about your wife? Or the motel guests? Does Lillie get along with them?"

"She and my wife are all right together. They're not good friends, mind you, but they get along just fine. The guests are a different story. Lillie's better than good with them. She treats them real friendly-like. If you ask me, it's because she knows her business depends on it. She may be a bit of a flirt, but she's not stupid."

"Were Lillie and Jake good together?"

"Now that's a good question," Ike said. "And I can't quite answer it. If you ask me, though, I'd say he should have left her years ago, right after she lost the baby. As far as I could see, that was the only reason Jake married her in the first place. To save her reputation, such as it was. For all I know, maybe it wasn't even his kid. Jake really loved children. He always wanted a big family. It hurt him bad to learn that Lillie couldn't have any more. I never understood why he stayed with her after that."

"True love, perhaps?" I suggested.

That made Ike laugh out loud. "I suppose anything's possible. All I know is that they worked well enough together running the motel. He took care of the handyman stuff. She dealt with the guests."

"How did they spend their time when they weren't working?" I asked.

"Mostly watching old movies on TV. I guess they had to do something with their evenings. Things get pretty quiet around here once the sun goes down. And when you're watching TV you don't have to talk much."

A pick-up hauling a mud-stained blue trailer pulled up to a gas pump. Ike jumped to attention. "Sorry. Duty calls. I'll be right back."

While Ike was pumping gas, I did a mental review of what he had told me so far. It was interesting enough, but there was no real smoking gun. I watched as Ike finished pumping gas and taking the trucker's credit card, then steeled myself for asking the one question that mattered the most.

Ike scanned the area as he walked back my way. No more vehicles looking for gas. No customers heading into the convenience store. He rejoined me in the parking area. "While the station is quiet, I need to get busy stocking the shelves in the store. The delivery came in late yesterday. I don't want to leave it sitting for my wife to worry about. Anything else you need to ask me before I go?"

Subtle wasn't his best trick, but I could live with that. "I just have a few more questions," I told him.

"Shoot," he said.

"Did you know the trucker who was shot?"

"Lou Bancroft? Sure. He's been coming around here for ages."

"What was he like?"

Ike shrugged. "Like anybody else, I suppose. Nice enough guy. Took care of his business. Kept to himself."

"Were he and Jake friends?"

"Not so you'd notice. I mean, they knew each other, but that was all."

"Do you know of any reason why someone would want to kill Lou?"

Ike shook his head. "Sorry."

I was sorry too. "One last thing," I said. "Do you think your brother might have killed himself?"

Ike's entire body stiffened. He gave me a long, cold stare. "Hell no. Jake liked his life. He deserved a whole lot better than what he got, but he sure as hell wasn't suicidal. And that's all I've got to say to you. Gotta get back to work."

He didn't actually say "So why don't you just write a check for his life insurance and be on your way?" But I heard it anyway. My unspoken answer to him was "Because we owe it to Jake to learn what really happened. And my boss would be furious if I paid a claim based on an inconclusive coroner's report. He'd also be unhappy if I were to spend too much time out here in the back of beyond. I'd worry about that tomorrow."

Chapter 23

Saturday, Afternoon / evening

I thanked Ike for his time and left him to tend to his business. It was mid-afternoon. I was pretty sure Pete wouldn't be back so early. I checked the room to confirm this. He was nowhere to be seen. OK. What to do next?

The answer to that was a no-brainer. It was a beautiful spring Saturday afternoon in rural Tennessee. I had put in a very full week on my case. My brain was over-full and needed a chance for things to settle. It was definitely time to have a little fun.

I jumped into my rented Mustang, put the top down and headed out for a joy ride. The air was cool and fresh and carried with it a hint of lavender. Just what I needed to lift my spirits and calm my mind. The country roads were lush and lovely, green with whatever spring crops they grow in Tennessee. My guess was lettuce or kale, but what did I know? I was more of a city person.

The roads I chose were both quiet and nicely straight—a delightful combination. Driving fast required less effort. I tuned the radio to a rock station, turned the volume up high and proceeded to exceed the speed limit—all the while clearing my mind of anything to do with life insurance, double shootings or tiny towns in the south. Sometimes that was the best way for me to solve things. As a rule, all manner of interesting ideas tended to pop into my mind when least expected.

After an hour or so of fresh air, high speed and glorious relaxation, I turned the Mustang around and headed back toward Hog Jaw. My phone chose that moment to ring, pulling me out of my reverie.

It was Peggy.

I pulled over to the side of the road to take the call. "How's my favorite dog-sitter?" I said. "Please don't tell me you're in the office on yet another Saturday."

She laughed. "No way. It's a gorgeous day in Cambridge. I don't want to miss a minute of it. My good friend Sam and I have just returned from a delightful stroll-and-sniff around the neighborhood. By the way, he says hello."

"Give him a big hug for me," I said. "Tell him I miss him and will be home soon."

"Will do."

"I hope he's being a good guest," I added. "And not causing you any trouble."

"Trouble, no," Peggy responded. "Mischief, yes."

Oh dear. That sounded vaguely ominous. "Explain."

"As you know, he spends a lot of time in my back yard," she began. "He loves it out there. I'm so glad I fenced it in. That gives Sam the chance to run a bit more freely and explore his world. He sure is one curious dog."

I couldn't argue with that. "Has he discovered anything of interest?"

"Not yet," Peggy said. "But he sure is trying to. He has taken to digging in the ground along the side of the picket fence. A lot. I don't know if he's searching for buried treasure or trying to carve out a tunnel under the fence and into the neighbor's yard. I fill it back in every day. And he digs it out again the first chance he gets."

That wasn't a surprise. Sam always loved to dig. "Is there anything in the neighbor's yard that might be worth the effort?" I asked.

"Some wild mushrooms popped up there a few days ago. They seem to have captured his attention."

Oh dear! "Can you tell if they're the poisonous kind?"

"I can," she said. "And they aren't. I'm hoping they're not the magic variety either. The thought of a psychedelic Sam is a little scary."

I held my breath and fought the urge to interrupt.

"I left a note for the neighbors asking if it would be all right for me to dig them up," she continued. "They're nice. I can't imagine they'd say no."

"Let's hope so," I said. "I'm not sure how soon I'll be home."

"Does that mean the case isn't going well?" she asked.

I wasn't sure how to answer that. The best I could come up with was: "I'm not quite sure. I'll let you know in a few days."

Before I could ask Peggy about goings-on in the office, her doorbell rang. "I've got company," she said. "Gotta go." And for once, we actually ended a conversation without even a minimal business discussion. That was a nice change. We could get back to life, death and insurance in Hog Jaw on Monday.

I put the Mustang back into gear and pulled back out onto the road.

It was late afternoon by the time I arrived back at the motel. Pete was in our room—on the phone. He ended the call quickly when he spotted me at the door, then smiled up at me. "Welcome back, Ames. How was your day?"

"Fine. Thanks. Who was that on the phone?" I asked.

"Oh, nobody important," he replied. "Just some business. I sure am hungry from hiking in the woods. Are you up for an early dinner at the diner?"

Nice segue, Buddy. If that call was business, apparently it was none of mine. Not in the mood to argue, I bit my tongue and said "Sure. Let's go."

The Saturday night crowd had already arrived ahead of us. There were a few truckers at the counter and two tables of Armstrong employees. A family with three young kids, all freckle-faced and redheaded, occupied the largest table. Must have been the children's weekend treat. Or Mom's night off. The kids seemed to be well-behaved—so far anyway.

Walt Taylor once again greeted us like old friends, or at least regular customers. For better or for worse, he wasn't wrong about that. Oh well, the place was convenient, the food was good and being there allowed me to observe the Hog Jaw denizens.

"How're you folks doing today?" Walt asked as he ushered us to our usual spot, a small table by the window. "Sure hope you're enjoying this fine weather. Make yourselves comfortable here and I'll get you some drinks. Will you be having the usual?"

We nodded, happy that this tiny out-of-the way place carried our "usuals."

Minnie approached our table with a frown she made no attempt to hide. There was a gravy stain on her black armband. "Special tonight's meatloaf," she droned, "same as every Saturday. What do you say?"

I flashed her my best smile. "I say fine, thank you. That sounds wonderful."

Pete dittoed that.

"I'm surprised to find you people still here," Minnie continued. "I expected that you would have paid the life insurance claim and gone on your way by now. I just don't understand what's holding everything up."

"I'm still working on a couple of things," I told her. "With any luck, it should all be wrapped up shortly." I hoped I wasn't lying to the woman.

Minnie grunted at that and lumbered off toward the kitchen mumbling something about luck not having anything to do with life insurance.

"She's not entirely wrong you know," Pete said, carefully avoiding my eyes in the process. "It is taking a slightly inordinate amount of time for such a small claim."

I was dangerously close to resenting that remark. "It's important for me to get this right, Pete. NEC&I can't afford to be paying out large sums on questionable claims."

"Yeah, right," he said. "I get that, still …"

"Still nothing," I snapped.

Walt arrived with our drinks before I could complete that thought. I used the pause in the conversation to put my case on mental hold for a while and to play nice instead.

"Why don't you tell me about your day?" I said to Pete.

"Sure. Why not?" He raised his glass. "Here's to a lovely Saturday evening in the back of beyond."

"How was Shaman Thomas?" I asked. "Did he show you his mushroom factory?"

Pete shook his head. "I'm afraid not. He texted me shortly before we were supposed to meet and said he wouldn't be able to make it today and could we put it off until Monday."

"Did he say why?"

"No."

I wondered if Pete had even asked. He was nowhere near as nosy as me, even when he was in his official lawyer persona. The poor guy had no clue what he might be missing.

Pete furrowed his brow, then added. "The funny thing is I could swear I saw him on the mountain a little while later."

"On Hog Jaw Mountain?"

"Yeah."

"Doing what?" I asked.

"Talking to some guys on the trail. I couldn't quite tell if they were hikers or bikers. I only saw them at a distance. At least I thought it was Shaman Thomas. I watched them for a few moments. Then they all took off, and disappeared down the other side of the mountain."

"Maybe it wasn't even him," I suggested.

Pete shrugged. "Whatever. Maybe I'll ask him about it when I see him on Monday."

That was doubtful. The Pete I knew and loved wouldn't want to pry.

"So what did you do up there all afternoon?" I asked.

Pete leaned toward me with his elbows on the table. "Well, let's see … I checked in with the office. Just to see if there was anything that needed my attention."

"On a Saturday?" I asked. "Was Moira actually there?"

"She was."

"Does she usually work on Saturdays?"

Pete avoided my eyes. "Off and on," he said. "It depends on what's going on. Sometimes she hangs out there to study or do an assignment for the class she's taking. It helps her to have access to my law books."

I wondered if the poor girl had any life outside of work. Oh well, not my business. At least I didn't think it was. "And what else did you do?"

"Made a few notes on what I need to do when I get back to the office. Then I read for a while. The book I brought it really good. I'll give it to you when I'm done if you want." He paused as Minnie delivered our meals without comment, then continued, "It's a mystery. I think you'd enjoy it."

I sampled my meatloaf. It was not as good as my mother's, but pretty tasty all the same. "So you sat on a log and read all afternoon?" I had trouble buying that scenario.

Pete shook his head. "Not really. I did a little hiking. Checked out those old tombstones that had fallen over. They were from the late 1800s. Marcus and Alice Taylor. So I guess somebody did live on the mountain at one time. Other than that, I mostly just sat and daydreamed."

Daydreamed? Pete? Now that was a first. I gave him a questioning look. "Really?"

"Yeah. Well … it seemed preferable to coming back here and hanging out in the motel room waiting for you to be done for the day."

Oh dear! That hit home—and it hurt. "Why didn't you call me? Or text? We could have done something together."

Instead of responding to that, Pete concentrated on his meatloaf. Finally he said, "I figured you'd be busy somewhere working on something to do with your case."

Part of me wanted to respond, "*Right. It's called working on my case. Which is why we're here.*" Another part of me silently asked myself "*Am I putting the job ahead of my time with Pete? And, if so, why?*" Aloud, I said, "How about I take tomorrow off and you and I take a trip to Memphis? Have some ribs, listen to some music. What do you say?"

Chapter 24

Sunday

I was determined to put everything to do with Hog Jaw out of my mind and devote the entire day to Pete on Sunday. My motivation may have been somewhat suspect. I knew for sure I loved the guy and wanted to be with him. I also knew I was feeling more than a little guilty about leaving him to fend for himself so much since we arrived in Hog Jaw. In the past, we had always enjoyed joining forces to tackle my more interesting cases, particularly when travel was involved. Something was different this time. Something I may have been reluctant to admit.

At any rate, we ate an early breakfast and headed west, eager to spend as much time as we could in Memphis. By way of compromise, we planned to take back roads on the way there so we could see something of rural west Tennessee. Pete wasn't quite sure why I wanted to do this. I sort of insisted. We could take the interstate on the return trip. It would be dark by then. There'd be nothing to see.

We gassed up the rented Mustang at Ike's garage and put the top down. It was a beautiful early spring morning. Sunday traffic was light. Life felt pretty damn good.

Less than half an hour into the trip, Pete turned to me and smiled. "I'm glad we decided to take this route instead of the interstate. This is pretty nice—quiet, peaceful, beautiful in its own way. So different from Massachusetts. A whole lot greener. Not to mention quieter."

"Seeing it from a Mustang convertible, top down, doesn't hurt," I added.

"I can't argue with that," Pete laughed. "So tell me, other than Beale Street, what are you interested in seeing in Memphis?"

"There is one thing I want to see, or do actually, before we even get to Memphis," I announced.

"And that would be … ?"

"I want to wade in the Mississippi River," I said.

He gave me the look he saved for those times when he seemed to be wondering what, if anything, we actually had in common. "Any particular reason?"

"Promise you won't laugh if I tell you," I said.

"That's a tough one, but all right, if you insist. But this better be good."

"It's because of that old song, you know, the one that says 'It's a treat to beat your feet on the Mississippi Mud.' I'd like to see if that's true."

"You're nuts," he said. "Now I suppose you're going to tell me you've already found a place where you can do this."

"Of course I have. There's a state park just north of the city. It has a boat launch on the river. We can wade there. It'll be fun."

Pete shook his head, but had the good sense not to comment. He kept his attention on the road for a few moments. Eventually he said, "Anything else?"

"We could check out the National Civil Rights Museum and possibly the Rock & Soul Museum and still have plenty of time to spend on Beale Street."

"No Graceland?" he asked.

"I can live without that," I replied. "Elvis was a bit before my time. Besides, Beale Street is the main attraction today. We want to leave plenty of time for that."

A few hours later, we were sitting in the brick-paved courtyard of a blues club on Beale Street, listening to fabulous live music and drinking beer, something I seldom do. I made an exception because beer seemed to be the best accompaniment to ribs.

This club was our third and final stop for the day. We had taken our time strolling around the three city blocks of restaurants, cafes and music which defined Beale Street. We had heard an eclectic mix of music along the way—blues, jazz, rock-n-roll, rhythm and blues and good old-fashioned gospel music. You name it; somebody played it. And it was all pretty great. We had finally settled in at an Irish pub which boasted of having the best ribs around. That was not to mention a cozy outdoor space with both live music and a view of the non-stop action on Beale Street. Not a bad way to spend what remained of the day.

I toasted Pete with my beer. "Today was fun. We must do this more often."

"It was a good time," he agreed. "So tell me, what was your favorite part?"

"Other than spending the entire day together, you mean?" I knew that sounded like sucking up, but I truly did mean it. And I was sort of sucking up as well. Whatever …

He nodded. "Right. What did you enjoy the most?"

I gave his question some serious thought before responding. "The Civil Rights Museum was wonderful. There was so much I never knew before, or perhaps forgot. And seeing the balcony where Martin Luther King was standing when he got shot brought more than one tear to my eyes."

"I know what you mean. I'm glad we went there."

"And what about you?" I asked. "What was your favorite part?"

Without a moment's hesitation, he answered, "Sitting here right now—drinking beer, waiting for ribs and listening to fabulous music."

I had hoped he'd add something about spending the day with me. No such luck. Oh well, I guess I probably deserved that.

A semi-enormous plate of ribs arrived at our table. Pete dug in like a starving man. I resigned myself to getting my hands greasy and grabbed a rib as well. It was pretty tasty.

We sat in silence for a while, enjoying the music and devouring the ribs. After a while, the fellow singing took a break. Pete put the rib he was eating back on his plate and leaned in toward me. "I had an affair with Moira," he announced.

"I suspected as much," I said, looking him directly in the eyes. "Is it over?"

"It is."

I wasn't sure I believed him. "Even though she's still working for you?"

He shrugged. "What can I say? She does a good job. I need the help. But I assure you, it is definitely over."

I sat back and watched him, curious to hear what he might say next.

Eventually he added, "So now we're even."

That wasn't what I expected to hear. When I regained control of myself, I asked, "What do you mean 'even'?"

"You know. Last fall. That cowboy. What was his name?"

I almost choked. "His name was Lance. And I assure you, I did not have an affair with the man."

Disbelief clouded Pete's eyes. "Really? It sure seemed that way to me. I saw the way he looked at you."

I began to feel defensive. "I had no control over how Lance looked at me. I say again: we did not have an affair."

"But you wanted to," Pete countered. "You at least thought about it."

He had me there. "Nevertheless …" I began.

He cut me off. "Nevertheless nothing. Remember Jimmy Carter committing lust in his heart?"

I didn't know how to respond to that. I was in no mood to argue. As good as I was about being confrontational on the job, personal matters were a whole different world. And I wasn't at all good at dealing with them. For the moment, I was too distraught to think straight. I simply said, "Thoughts and actions are two different things. And I definitely controlled *my* actions." *So there!*

After a bit, I pulled myself together enough to say, "I love you, Pete. I thought you knew that."

No response.

That wasn't good.

We sat in silence and gnawed on ribs. The music started up again, at just about the time I felt my world as I knew it might be ending.

After what seemed like forever, Pete finally said, "I love you too, Ames. And I do want to make this work. We're good together on so many levels."

"So where do we go from here?" I finally choked out. This was difficult for me. I was never very good at being vulnerable. "I'd like to give it another try. Just move on from here. What do you say?"

He gave that some serious thought before responding, "I'm willing to give it a try," he finally told me, then added, "But we've got to be totally honest and open with each other from now on. No holding back. Agreed?"

"Agreed."

We lapsed into what seemed to me to be relieved silence as we finished our ribs and concentrated on the music.

Chapter 25

Monday morning

Pete and I slept late Monday morning. Actually, sleep had very little to do with it. Rather, we devoted some time to rekindling the romance that had always been an important part of our relationship. It had fallen by the wayside over the past few months. Getting it back was important if we were ever going to make things right between us. At the moment, it was working just fine.

After a late breakfast, Pete headed off to the mountain to meet with Shaman Thomas. I was actually glad to see him go. As much as I cared for the guy, and as helpful as he often was with my investigations, there were also times when he was more of a distraction that a help. Today was one of those days. I had been in Hog Jaw an entire week now. NEC&I really couldn't afford to have me spending much more time on one small case.

The trouble was that it was against my nature to leave any stone unturned or any question unanswered. And I still had questions.

I steeled myself to get back to work. I had an early afternoon appointment at the sheriff's office with the widow of Lou Bancroft, the other fellow who was shot that night. She was coming from her home in Kansas to retrieve her late husband's body, which had just been released for burial.

I was clinging to a vague and probably unsubstantiated hope that she'd have something interesting to tell me that would solve my entire case.

Nevertheless, settling down to work required some serious effort. The morning was warm and sunny, with just the hint of a breeze. I liked the fact that spring came a lot earlier in Tennessee than it did in Boston. Maybe that was part of the reason I wasn't in any great hurry to get home. This morning, I came up with a way to work outside, even if it was only on the walkway outside an old motel in Hog Jaw, TN. I didn't care about the noise of trucks back-firing or the subtle scent of exhaust fumes coming from the nearby interstate. I didn't care about what the residents of Hog Jaw thought. I simply couldn't remain in the motel room. I was nearly finished packing up my laptop when my phone rang.

So much for fresh air and sunshine.

It was Peggy.

Maybe she'd have some interesting information to help jump start my day.

Instead of a greeting, she began with "Are you no longer checking your email in the morning now? I expected to hear back from you well over an hour ago."

"What can I say?" I replied. "I got caught up in something else."

"Anything you want to tell me about?" she teased.

"Maybe later," I lied. "Hold on a minute while I get my laptop up and running. Motel rooms provide notoriously awkward desks." I settled myself in as best I could, then asked, "So, what's up? How is life today at good old NEC&I?"

Peggy laughed and said, "My life is just fine, both on and off the job. However, I'm not so sure about Tiffany's. From what I can see, she didn't have much of anything going on over the weekend. It looks like she spent most of it delving into the dark web on your case."

That was more than a little disturbing—even though she was researching something helpful to my case. "Explain."

"Things got a little crazy for me here last Friday," Peggy began. "Nothing you need to worry about, just a lot of annoying busy work that hit my desk all at once. I asked Tiffany if she might have some time to research the Brave Hearts. I had already done some preliminary work, so it gave her a head start."

"And?" I asked. "I'm guessing you ladies came up with something of interest."

"You're guessing correctly," Peggy said. "And it's better than merely interesting. It's more like something totally untoward."

"OK. Let's have it."

"I'll give you the easy stuff first. Per both Google and Facebook, there are a number of organizations using the name Brave Hearts. One is a healing horsemanship program for troubled adults. Another is a religious group dedicated to assisting people in recovery. I'm not quite sure from what. There's even a hip hop group that uses the name. Then there's the motorcycle club. And that's where things get interesting."

"How so?" I asked.

"First of all, they're nationwide, and fairly large," she told me. "There's a local chapter in at least three dozen states. Both their website and their Facebook page are pretty innocuous, bordering on the boring and the banal." That confirmed what Snow had told me.

I smiled to myself. I also wondered if Peggy had put in some time reading her thesaurus over the weekend. She definitely did have a way with words.

When Peggy came up for air, she continued, "Tiffany hit paydirt. Don't ask me what she did or how she did it, but that girl certainly does work in mysterious ways. I'm wondering if she has an affiliation with somebody on the dark web or something equally ominous. Her ability to locate arcane information is more than a little unsettling. It's no wonder George is out to get her. I'm thinking she probably scares him."

I sat up a little straighter, waiting for the punch line. "What did she find?"

"The Brave Hearts are indeed a motorcycle club. That part is totally legit, but it is also a cover for their other activities. They are a hate group," Peggy said. "They're racist and sexist bullies determined to destroy democracy, and probably life as we know it. Based on what Tiffany found, these guys make groups like the Proud Boys look like boy scouts."

I held my breath as I digested this information. When I was able to speak, all I could manage to say was "Holy shit."

"Holy shit and then some," Peggy continued. "But wait. There's more. And you're not going to believe it."

"What?"

"Somehow, somewhere, Tiffany came across rantings posted by some of the members. Disturbing things. And more than once, these posts were signed, or at least attributed by name to various members. Tiff then began digging for anything she could find on those members. And … are you ready for this? Please tell me you're sitting down."

I was running short of patience at this point. "Just tell me, please. Now."

"Two of them work for Armstrong Industries."

I dropped my phone on the floor.

Once recovered, and reseated at the desk, I said, "So you're telling me there may be domestic terrorists making bombs in Tennessee."

"I'm afraid so."

My day just got a whole lot more interesting. And perhaps a bit scary.

Then another thought struck me, sort of like a ton of bricks, only worse. I mulled it over for a few moments, then said to Peggy, "The problem I now have is that my actual mission in Tennessee is to investigate, and most likely pay, Jake Taylor's life insurance claim. It's not to involve myself with motorcycle clubs or radical hate groups who manufacture bombs."

"Stop right there," Peggy said. She could be very bossy at times. "I have a question. And I need an honest answer."

"Shoot."

"What is it you always tell me about coincidence?"

"There's no such thing," I said. "And I'm right. There isn't."

"Bingo! And what does that mean?"

In the end, the answer to that was a no-brainer. "It means that I'd like to speak with the folks at Armstrong Industries, as soon as possible," I said. "Can you arrange that for me? I'm tied up all day tomorrow. Please see if you can set something up for Wednesday."

She hesitated for just a moment. "What shall I give them as the reason for your visit?"

That was easy. "Tell them I need to speak with everybody who was in the area of the Hog Jaw Motel on or around the day of the shooting. I see enough of their employees at the diner to make that plausible. Play it up big if you have to. You know, something like 'Poor Lillie, left to run the motel all by herself. Poor Walter and Minnie who run the diner. Their son was killed. We'd like to help them get some closure.' Or something to that effect. Can do?"

"Can do," Peggy replied. "I'll get back to you later with the details."

"I'll look forward to it," I told her. "Is there anything else before I go?"

"Just one thing. I finally managed to track down Dick Greene."

"The other trucker who was at the Hog Jaw Motel the night of the shooting?" I asked.

"Right. We spoke this morning. He seemed like a nice guy. He's on the road all week but would be happy to speak with you over the phone."

That was good news. Peggy gave me Greene's number and we ended the call. I texted Dick Greene to arrange for a time to speak with him. He responded right away. Today didn't work well for him. We arranged a time to connect tomorrow morning.

I texted him back to confirm, then checked the time. Nearly noon. Just about enough time to update my notes before heading out to the Sheriff's office.

Chapter 26

Monday afternoon

The ride to the sheriff's office consisted of about thirty minutes of windy roads and glorious sunshine—and the top down on my rented Mustang. I arrived in an upbeat state of mind, ever hopeful that I was about to make the break-through that would wrap up my investigation. I wanted to present Lillie Taylor with a check for $500,000. I truly did. But I also wanted to learn what had really happened that night. On some level, I probably needed that for my own peace of mind. I hoped that Lou Bancroft's widow would help.

The Bryant County municipal building loomed large and proud in the Humboldt town square. Besides the sheriff's office, it also contained both the county courtroom and the jail. Sort of like one-stop shopping. Not bothering to lock the car, I headed in to meet with Lou Bancroft's widow. Sheriff Snow greeted me at the door.

"Good afternoon, Ms. Lynch. Welcome to my domain, such as it is. Please come this way. Mrs. Bancroft is waiting to speak with you."

"Thank you for making this possible," I said as I followed Snow through a doorway on the left and into a small office.

A youngish woman dressed in a faded denim skirt, a white blouse in need of ironing and a navy-blue cardigan two sizes too big for her rose to greet me. She was tall, thin and tired-looking, with limp hair, pale skin and sad eyes. Everything about her screamed "Poor thing." My heart went out to her.

The sheriff made the introductions, then asked, "Do you ladies mind if I stick around while you chat?"

I replied, "Not at all." Mrs. Bancroft nodded her assent.

"Thank you so much for agreeing to speak with me, Mrs. Bancroft," I said.

"Please, call me Doreen. Mrs. Bancroft is my witch of a mother-in-law."

I nodded. "Then Doreen it is. I'm Amy. Please accept my condolences on the death of your husband. I'm sure this is all very difficult for you." My words sounded cliché to the point of being meaningless, no matter how much I actually meant them.

She responded with a half-hearted "Thanks."

"Do you mind if I record this?" I asked as I pulled out my phone.

Doreen sank into a chair and sighed. "Sure. No problem."

I hit the record button and began, "For the record, your late husband, Lou Bancroft, was a trucker. Correct?"

"Yes," she murmured. "Ever since we got married and the babies started coming."

"What did he do before that?"

She stared blankly at a stain on the ceiling. "He was a soldier when I met him. So handsome in his uniform."

"Which branch?" I asked.

"Marines. Special ops," she replied. "He did a couple of tours In Afghanistan. My Lou was a sniper. He was really good with guns."

• That got my attention—big time. I couldn't help but ask her, "Did he give up guns when he left the service?"

Doreen shook her head. "No. Not really."

I wasn't quite sure what that meant. "Did he carry a firearm?"

"He did. Pretty much all the time," she told me. "It was part of who he was, I think. He seemed a bit lost without one."

The sheriff spoke up at this point. "What type of firearm did your husband carry, Ma'am? A pistol or a rifle?"

"Rifle. Always a rifle. He left the pistol at home with me, for protection when he was on the road."

"Was he licensed to carry?" Sheriff Snow asked.

Doreen shrugged and avoided the sheriff's eyes. "In some states."

The sheriff frowned. "Not a good idea. I guess it doesn't matter much anymore, though. And the great state of Tennessee doesn't require a license for a firearm used for home defense."

Doreen nodded her head. Snow's shoulders relaxed.

I wondered if "home defense" extended to his truck.

"Did your husband own more than one pistol?" I asked Doreen. "Perhaps one for you at home and one for himself on the road?"

"I don't think so," she said. "I only ever saw the one."

"Are you sure he left it home with you when he went on the last trip?" I continued.

"Absolutely. I always made sure of that."

And yet Lou had a pistol in his hand the night he was killed. Sheriff Snow and I exchanged questioning glances, but neither of us spoke up.

"Let's talk about your husband being on the road," I suggested. "Was he gone a lot?"

"I'm afraid so," she answered with a frown. "As much as we hated it, we had no real choice. Long-haul trucking pays better than any local job. We needed the money. Sometimes he was gone four or five days a week. That made it hard for me, alone at home with four small kids. The oldest is only ten. I couldn't get a job. It would cost me more to pay for day care than I could earn anywhere." She let out a long, sad sob. "I don't know what I'm going do now."

I fought the urge to pat her on the back and say that everything would be all right. It probably wouldn't be. Better to return to the business at hand. I gave her a few moments to regain her composure, then continued, "Did Lou have a regular route?"

Doreen nodded. "For the most part, yeah. He also took any extra runs he could manage to fit in."

"Did he often pass through Hog Jaw?"

"Pretty much every week. It was a good stopping-off point. And the motel there was always clean, and not too expensive."

"Did he get to know the people there?" I asked.

"Yeah. Sure. I guess so. I mean, he must have, right?"

"Were he and Jake Taylor friends?"

Doreen gave that some thought. "He talked about Jake. They knew each other. I don't know if you'd say exactly friends, though. Lou usually dealt with Lillie."

"Were he and Lillie friends?"

"Not as friendly as she wanted to be. When Lou first began staying there, she sort of came on to him, but he wasn't interested. He ignored her advances, kept things all business all the time."

Or so he said. I decided to let that subject go, at least for the time being. "I'm guessing he saw a lot of the same truckers there over time," I suggested. "It seems like a popular stopping off place, being right off the interstate."

"Yeah. Right. A lot of them knew each other. Sometimes they ate together in the diner. Long haul trucking can get lonely, you know."

"Did they all get along?" I asked.

Doreen shrugged. "Sure, as far as I know. Why not?"

I took a moment to search my brain, certain I was missing something. Finally, I asked, "What about the local Hog Jaw residents? Did Lou have much contact with any of them?"

Doreen let out a little laugh. "Hog Jaw residents? There sure weren't many of those. From what Lou told me, there was just Lillie and Jake at the motel, the gas station guy and his wife and the couple who run the diner."

She fell silent for a moment and wrinkled her brow. "Hey, wait a minute. Now that I think about it, there were some other people. Lou saw them in the woods."

My phone jumped out of my hands and into my lap. "In the woods?" I asked. "What was Lou doing in the woods?"

"He was taking a walk. I remember it now. He told me all about it."

I retrieved my phone, still recording, and waited for Doreen to continue.

She did. "Lou was a real country boy. Loved the out-of-doors. He was also an early-morning person. When he was on the road, he liked to get an early start. Less traffic that way. He liked to stop for the day by mid-afternoon. Whenever possible, he'd take a walk then after he'd check into a motel. He said it helped to get the kinks out from sitting in the rig for so long. And to keep himself from falling asleep before dinner and then being awake half the night. He was particularly fond of Hog Jaw for this reason. He could head for the woods nearby and hike up to the top of the mountain there and be back in plenty of time for dinner at the diner."

"And he said he met somebody there?" I prompted.

"Sort of, yeah. Lou told me he ran across a couple of guys there a week or so ago. He said they looked like they were up to no good."

Sheriff Snow broke in here. "Define 'no good' please."

"Lou thought it might be a drug deal," Doreen said. "One of them handed something to the other guy. Something sort of big and bulky. Lou couldn't see what. Then the second guy gave the first one some money." She bit her lip for a moment, then added, "Then they noticed Lou."

Big and bulky didn't sound much like drugs to me. But at the moment I couldn't imagine what it might be. "Did they say anything to him?" I asked.

"Oh boy, did they ever," she replied. "Lou told me that one of them, a scruffy looking guy with a beard went after him. Threatened him. Told him he better not tell anybody what he thought he saw. Or else."

"Or else what?" asked Snow. "And why is this the first I'm hearing about this? Lou should have reported the incident."

"Probably because he was afraid," Doreen said. "That same guy showed up at the diner that night when Lou was having dinner. He didn't say anything to Lou, just sat there and glared at him, real mean like. Lou got the message."

Oh dear! That was disturbing on so many levels. Maybe it wasn't safe for Pete to be spending time on the mountain. I needed to talk to him about that.

Chapter 27

Monday evening

"I hate to admit this," I said to Pete as we walked from our motel room to the Hog Jaw Diner, "but I may be getting sick of eating at the same place day after day, night after night."

"I know what you mean," he replied. "But it has been convenient, not to mention helpful to your case. And we won't be here much longer, right?"

I surely hoped that was the case. We had been in Tennessee an entire week now. Mark would want me back in the office sooner rather than later. That would be fine with me. A week was a long time for me in the back of beyond. I was a city girl at heart. And I was lonesome for my dog Sam. He was my friend and confidant. I often told him things even Peggy didn't know, not to mention Pete.

And I knew what Pete meant about the Hog Jaw Diner. It had worked out well for us so far. However, after dinner tonight we would have sampled all their nightly specials. Tonight was franks and beans. And the place was packed. Who knew it was such a popular dish?

Walt and Minnie, still wearing black armbands, were as cordial as ever, but didn't linger and chat with us. That was a relief. I hated telling them, again and again, that I wasn't quite ready to close my case and pay the life insurance claim.

While waiting for our meals to arrive, I sipped my wine and gave Pete a detailed rundown of my conversation with Lou Bancroft's wife. His back stiffened when I got to the part about Lou being threatened on Hog Jaw Mountain.

"What is it?" I asked.

His answer surprised me. "I'm beginning to believe that there's a lot more going on out there on that mountain than meets the eye."

Minnie chose that moment to deliver our meals. I forced a smile and a "Thank you" then waited for her to leave. "Explain that, please. In great detail."

After sampling his franks and beans, Pete put his elbows on the table and leaned in closer to me. Lowering his voice, he said, "I've seen more than a few shady-looking characters on that mountain. Definitely not your ordinary run-of-the-mill hikers. There's just something off about them. At first I thought it was simply my imagination on overdrive. Now I'm pretty sure that's not the case."

"Did something happen up there today?" I asked.

Pete's response was a resounding, "Sort of."

I gulped. "Please, tell me about it."

Pete took a deep breath and a moment to organize his thoughts. "Shaman Thomas was waiting for me in the hikers' parking area when I arrived there this morning. He had come on a motorcycle, which he promptly moved behind some bushes in the far end of the lot."

I gave that a moment's thought. "It sounds to me as if he didn't want the bike to be stolen."

"Maybe," Pete frowned. "Or maybe he didn't want it to be seen at all."

"Do you think you might be overreacting here?" I suggested.

"I might have thought so, if it hadn't been for what came next."

I stopped eating and gave him my full attention. "Which was …?"

"The shaman led me to the top of the mountain, but never on any of the regular hiking trails. We made our way through the woods by ways that were barely even paths. And any time he heard voices coming from the trails, he stopped dead still and shushed me. And there we stayed until all was quiet. When we started up again, he kept checking behind, as if to make sure we weren't being followed."

"Good lord," I said. "Is the mushroom growing activity at the top of the mountain all that big a deal?"

Pete nodded. "My question exactly. When I asked him about it, he reminded me the mound at the top was a sacred place for his people, reserved for rituals and tribal business. And that the mushrooms he grew there were an important part of those rituals. He couldn't allow any of that to be spoiled by outsiders."

"I can understand that."

"But wait," Pete said. "There's more."

I waited, but not for long.

"Let us not forget that what goes on up there is also totally illegal," Pete reminded me.

"Oh, right," I said. "Magic mushrooms are against the law. But isn't there some sort of exception for use in religious rituals?"

"In some states, yes. And for some substances. Like peyote in Texas. But that's pretty rare. Psilocybin is definitely outlawed in Tennessee."

I sat back and ran through a few things in my mind. "Is there any chance Shaman Thomas is overreacting to what could be simple curiosity on the part of the hikers?"

Pete shook his head. "No way. For whatever reason, Thomas truly believes that someone or something is threatening his domain. I could see it in his eyes." Pete paused, took a big swig of beer and added, "After that, the mushrooms themselves were an anti-climax."

"Tell me about them anyway," I said.

Before he could do so, a trio of what looked like truckers burst in through the door, accompanied by raucous laughter. They proceeded to greet just about everybody in the diner before settling down at the only available table. I was pretty sure Hog Jaw was part of their regular route.

Once the noise settled back down, Pete said, "Shaman Thomas grows the mushrooms in a cavern deep inside a system of caves. I don't know why that surprised me, but it did. The opening is well hidden. And we walked quite a long way before reaching the growing room.

The place was cold and dank. Not to mention dark. I was happy to see that the shaman had brought a flashlight. The mushrooms are growing all the way in the back of the cave. Fifteen rows of them, a dozen mushrooms in each row. All pretty much the same size. All lined up and waiting to be harvested."

"You counted them? Whatever for?"

He shrugged. "Curiosity, I suppose. Why not?"

I couldn't stop myself from asking, "Was there anything else in the cave? Perhaps a few bats or rats or something equally creepy?"

"Not that I could see."

"Did the shaman tell you much about the tribe's rituals?"

"Yes and no," Pete replied. "He didn't go into a great detail, but he did stress the importance to his people of preserving the old ways, not letting their heritage die. Then he got a little mystical and told me how the mushrooms can open minds to a variety of profound insights. He described it as heightening the senses to the spiritual world and reaching harmony with the universe. It sounded pretty cool to me."

I was a little surprised to hear the Pete I knew and loved admit that. "I remember reading somewhere that psilocybin mushrooms have medicinal value as well. Did Joseph say anything about that?" I asked.

Pete nodded. "Right. He said they have been used to treat conditions like depression and addiction. Also PTSD."

"You'd think it would be legal in more states for those purposes alone," I said. Then I couldn't help but ask, "Did you get to try the mushrooms?"

Pete gave me an exasperated look. "Please tell me you're kidding. I think you know me better than that."

Before I could respond, all hell broke loose in the diner. At least half of the patrons, all seemingly truckers, jumped up and dashed outside. A group of bikers met them in the parking lot, with fire in their eyes. The rest of the diners, except for Pete and me, crowded at the windows as an all-out brawl began.

Minnie and Walt remained behind the counter, shaking their heads. "Here they go again," Minnie said. "These guys need to learn to get along somehow. This brawling is getting to be a regular occurrence. Do you think it's about time for us to call the sheriff?"

Walt shook his head. "Looks like it might not be necessary. At least not tonight. Things are quieting down. A couple of guys are heading to their rigs."

"Let's hope they've already paid their bills," Minnie scowled. "This is beginning to get out of hand. It's bad for business."

Walt and Minnie and Pete and I watched as folks came back into the diner.

Minnie shook her head and said, "I wish those folks had never come here."

She disappeared into the kitchen before I could ask her which folks she meant, and why.

Chapter 28

Tuesday morning

It was yet another beautiful spring day. I was beginning to wonder if it ever rained in West Tennessee. And happy it hadn't done so this past week.

Pete and I were on our way to Nashville. Technically, the purpose of the trip was for me to meet with a fellow named Gary Miller, a biker and wannabe singer. I was guessing that the man was part of the Brave Heart bikers' group. That made me a little uncomfortable after what Peggy had told me about them. I was glad to have Pete with me. And, spending the day in Nashville was a nice bonus. I loved it when I got to combine business with pleasure. Pete had been to Nashville before; I had not.

I decided to wear my pale blue dress with the matching jacket, business casual at its best. I needed to look somewhat professional for a day in the big city. I did not, however, wear heels. At Miller's request, Pete was sporting a Red Sox cap. It would make us easy to spot. Oddly enough, Pete had brought one with him. Every once in a while, the guy managed to surprise me.

As usual, Pete did the driving. We took the interstate so we could have as much time as possible in the city. That was all right with me even if it did mean we couldn't put the top down. I could get some work done along the way. Specifically, I was doing a telephone interview with Dick Greene, the other trucker who had been at the Hog Jaw Motel on the night in question.

Once Greene and I connected, I put the phone on speaker and grabbed a notebook and pen. I began with the easy stuff. "I really appreciate you taking the time to speak me, particularly when you're on the road."

"No big deal," he said. "I'm on a major highway, which means easy driving. And I'm happy to help you any way I can. Jake was a good guy."

"What can you tell me about the night of the shooting?" I asked.

Greene's first response was a long, loud sigh. Finally, he said, "Not a whole lot, I'm afraid. I had just fallen asleep. I had been up late talking to my wife and kids on the phone. I heard a siren really close by. I ran out my door, saw Lillie crying and wailing outside of room 8. The sheriff was just arriving. The ambulance too. I didn't really know what was going on at first. Then somebody, can't say as I even remember who, filled me in. It was awful, just awful. I had a hard time believing it was real."

"So you didn't hear anything earlier? Like perhaps a gunshot?" I asked.

"Nope. Like I said, I was on the phone, then asleep. Sorry."

"What did you do when you went outside?"

"There wasn't much I could do," he told me. "I gave my name and number to the Sheriff then did my best to stay out of everybody's way. I heard somebody say that it was Jake's body they were bringing out. That almost made me want to cry."

Greene paused as if to pull himself together. I waited with as much patience as I could muster.

Finally, he said, "And that's about it, I'm afraid. I hung around outside of my room and watched until the ambulance left and things calmed down. I'm truly sorry I'm not able to be of more help to you."

That wasn't necessarily so. I suspected he might be able to provide me with some helpful background information on the cast of characters involved. Might as well give it a shot. "Were you and Jake friends?" I asked. "Did you know him well?"

"I guess you could say we were friends. Of a sort, anyway. I've been staying at the Hog Jaw Motel for years now. Usually twice a week, Thursdays and Sundays. It fits right into my regular route. Jake always made me feel welcome. We got to hanging out together over a beer in the evening, just passing the time. Like I said, he was a good guy. And he sure deserved a whole lot better than he got."

I sat up a little straighter. "What do you mean?"

"Well," Greene replied, "you know, I hate to go telling tales on anybody, or speaking ill of them, but ..."

But what Dick? Spill it. I'm all ears.

"It's that Lillie, his wife."

"What about Lillie?" I prompted.

"That gal is something else, and none of it is good. She's nothing but a floozie as far as I'm concerned. More than once I saw her spending more time with those darn bikers than she did with Jake. Hanging out with them in the parking lot, laughing and having a grand old time. I don't know how Jake put up with it, or why."

"Did Jake ever discuss it with you?" I asked.

"He never said a word to me about Lillie, good or bad," Greene said. "He'd watch her sometimes, though, with a sad look in his eye. Like I said, I felt bad for the guy."

I couldn't help but feel the same way. "What about the bikers? Did Jake say much about them?"

"Sure did. All the time. He hated the lot of them. They were nothing but trouble as far as he was concerned. He didn't trust them worth a lick."

"And yet he put up with them. They spend a lot of time in Hog Jaw," I said. "From what I've been told, they're there most every weekend."

"True enough. And sometimes during the week as well. Jake hated every minute of it. He couldn't stop it, though. Couldn't afford to. They were regular customers. They paid cash. He needed them to keep the place going."

I had to ask: "Was there any animosity between Jake and the bikers? Did you ever see them arguing with Jake? Or giving him a hard time?"

"I can't say that I did. From what I saw, Jake mostly just plain avoided them. Kept his distance as much as possible."

I wasn't all that surprised by what Dick Greene was telling me. It was more like confirming what I had suspected. I wondered what other interesting tidbits this guy might have for me. "Do you know any of the other truckers who stop in Hog Jaw regularly?"

He answered without any hesitation. "A couple of them, yeah. Life gets a mite lonely on the road, you know. It's always nice to see a familiar face, maybe share a table in the diner with a fellow road warrior. It sure beats eating alone night after night."

"Did you know Lou Bancroft?" I asked.

"Lou? Sure. He was in Hog Jaw almost as much as me. We sit together at the counter in the diner a lot. Or rather, we did. I still can't believe he's gone. I sure am going to miss our dinnertime chats."

"What was Lou like?"

"I suppose he was an ordinary enough guy. Decent. Honest, as far as I could see. In the same boat as I was, needing to spend more time on the road than with our families in order to make life possible for them. Like I said, it gets lonely on the road. He told me all about his family. Lord, was he ever proud of his kids. I guess that life's about to get pretty tough for them now, with him gone. Some things just aren't fair, you know?"

I knew. "What else did you two talk about?"

Greene thought about that for a few moments. "Not a whole lot, I guess. Mostly just the everyday stuff - life on the road, what was for dinner, things like that. Oh, yeah, and hunting. That's the other thing he and I had in common. We both love to hunt. Lou used to bring his hunting rifle on the road with him sometimes and spend an hour or two hunting in the woods and hills around Hog Jaw whenever he arrived early enough in the day. I would have liked to join him doing that. Too late now. Too bad. It could've been fun."

Lou's widow hadn't mentioned anything about him spending time hunting in Hog Jaw. I had to wonder why. Did she even know about it? Did it even matter? "As far as you know, did Lou bring a pistol with him on the road?" I asked Greene.

"Nope," came the reply. "That can be a dangerous thing to do when you're crossing through multiple states. Laws are different everywhere. Most truckers don't want to take a chance of getting caught. Too many unpleasant consequences."

And yet Lou carried a rifle. I had to wonder why. I did a quick mental review to see if there was anything else I wanted to ask Dick Greene. Only one thing came to mind. "Was there any bad blood between Jake and Lou?"

Greene's response was a moment in coming. Finally, he said, "I don't believe so. At least nothing that I knew about."

That was good to know.

I thanked Dick Greene for his time and wished him well.

A text from Peggy had arrived while I was on the phone saying I had a 2:00 appointment on Wednesday with Edwin Tuttle at Armstrong Industries. She said he had agreed grudgingly and told her that he had no idea why I'd want to speak with him. I promised myself that I'd be on my best behavior. No point annoying folks who made bombs.

Then I sat back and closed my eyes, trying to work out how what Greene had told me fit in with everything else I had learned about the double shooting.

Chapter 29

Later Tuesday

W e arrived in Nashville a little after 10:00. I had a 1:00 meeting with Gary Miller. That gave me and Pete a couple of hours to explore Music City, USA. I was eager to get started right away so we could make the most of our time.

Parking was a bitch. We ended up on the third floor of an indoor parking lot. I've always hated indoor lots. Driving around inside just never felt right to me.

We went first to the Country Music Hall of Fame. It was a marvelous museum, made all the more interesting to me because I had recently seen the Ken Burns special on country music. We spent well over an hour there checking out a fascinating variety of recordings, videos, photos and instruments. It was fun to see things like Mother Maybelle's guitar and Earl Scruggs' banjo.

From there, we headed to the Ryman Auditorium, for many years the home of the Grand Ole Opry. The interior felt like a church, which apparently it was at one time. I particularly loved an enormous mural on a wall just outside the Ryman filled with portraits of country singers. I surprised myself with how many I could identify.

We took a long, slow stroll through the heart of downtown Nashville. We saw Tootsies Orchid Lounge and a few other well-known old Nashville haunts. Overall, though, a lot of it looked more like NashVegas than like the image I had in mind after seeing the Ken Burns documentary. There was music coming from nearly every club or restaurant that we passed. That was pretty nice, particularly in the middle of the day. It reminded me a bit of Beale Street in Memphis, but without the soul.

The restaurant where we were meeting Gary Miller was in the heart of downtown. It had outdoor seating, a nice treat on such a beautiful day. No afternoon music, though. Oh well, we could hear the entertainment from the bar across the street just fine.

Miller spotted us as soon as we sat down. He joined us at our table. The Red Sox cap had been a good idea. He was wearing one as well. He was young-looking, probably in his late twenties, blond, clean-shaven and casually yet conservatively dressed in jeans and a white tee shirt. The man didn't look much like a biker to me, let alone a militant terrorist. I crossed my fingers and hoped for the best.

After making introductions, I got right to work. "Thank you so much for agreeing to meet with us," I began. "Do you mind if I record this?"

The man shrugged. "Sure. Not a problem. And, by the way, thank you for driving all this way to chat," Miller said. "I start work at 3:00. That really cuts into my daytime leisure activities, but I need the job."

"I was happy to do so," I assured him. "It gave me a chance to visit Nashville and get paid for it."

A waiter arrived at our table with menus. We ordered drinks and told him we needed to think about what to eat.

Once he left, Miller sat back in his chair. "So, how can I help you folks?"

I took a deep breath, then began, "I understand that you were at the Hog Jaw Motel on the night of the shooting."

"That's right. It's part of my regular route when I'm on the open road. That part of the state is every biker's dream—long, winding roads, rolling hills, not much traffic. What more could a fellow want?"

"Are you a member of the Brave Hearts?" I held my breath as I waited for his response, not sure if I really wanted to know. Or if I actually wanted to deal with one of them after what Peggy had told me.

Miller shook his head. "I used to be. I quit them several years ago."

"Any particular reason?" I asked.

Miller closed his eyes and frowned. "Politics. They were becoming more and more extreme in their views. When they started talking about the upcoming changes and the part they hoped to play, I'd had enough. It wasn't like they were making big plans, at least not right away. But they were, as they put it, getting ready for what was going to happen. I didn't want to be a part of that. No way, thank you very much."

Pete looked appalled. "Did you tell this to the authorities? Any authorities?"

"Nope. Couldn't. Didn't dare. I kept telling myself it was all just talk and nothing would ever come of it. Just a bunch of middle-aged malcontents airing their grievances."

I hoped Miller was right about that. Still, I'd look into them a little deeper, just in case. "So you're no longer in touch with them?" I asked.

"Not really," was the response. "Their biking routes are great, though. I still use them every chance I get."

"Do you run into any Brave Hearts when you're riding out there?" Pete asked.

"Not often which is just fine with me. I tend to be out that way mostly mid-week, including an overnight whenever I get two days off in a row. I work here in Nashville most weekends. That's when the Brave Hearts usually ride."

I wanted to know more about him and the Brave Hearts, but decided I should get down to the business at hand first. "Do you often stay at the Hog Jaw Motel?"

He nodded. "Yeah. I've been going there for years. They're nice people. The rates are reasonable. What's not to love?"

"Can you tell me what you saw the night of the shooting? Or heard?"

"Not much, I'm afraid," he said, shaking his head. "The sirens woke me up."

I stopped him right there. "So you didn't hear any gunshots?"

He shook his head. "Nope. And if I did, I probably would have thought it was just a truck backfiring on the Interstate. Anyway, I stepped outside my door and into the chaos. Lillie was in hysterics. The sheriff was shouting and trying to keep people from getting too close to room 8. The EMTs came out of the room with a body on a stretcher. All covered up. Obviously dead. They got that stretcher into the ambulance, then went back into the room and came out a minute or two later with another stretcher, and another body. Folks were wondering who the victims were. Nobody knew for sure. It was a madhouse. I hung back as much as I could and tried see what was going on but still manage to keep from being noticed."

The waiter came by with our drinks. We ordered some lunch. Miller wanted a burger. Pete and I went for the ribs.

Once the waiter left, Miller continued, "The sheriff came over to us and said that nobody should leave without giving him their names and contact info. It took a while to get all that sorted out. After I spoke with the sheriff, I went back to my room and tried to get a little more sleep." He took a deep breath, then let it out slowly. "And that's about it. Sorry I can't be more helpful to you."

Not quite it, my friend. I still had some questions. "Why didn't you want to be noticed?" I asked.

Miller tightened his hands into fists and stared at them.

I pretended to wait patiently. Not always easy for me to do. Finally, I spoke up, "Was there somebody there you didn't want to deal with?"

He nodded, but said nothing.

"Who was it?" I pushed.

"A guy named Snake," he muttered. "That's who."

Pete put down his beer and decided to become part of the conversation. "You knew Snake from being a member of the Brave Hearts." It was a statement, not a question.

Miller scowled. "Right. And the son-of-a-bitch nearly ruined my life once. I wasn't about to give him a chance to try again."

I nearly choked on my wine. "How so?"

"He got me involved in some bad business," Miller replied.

I looked him in the eyes and waited for him to continue.

After a few moments, he added, "Moving drugs. On Hog Jaw Mountain."

Somehow, I wasn't surprised.

"Biggest mistake of my life," Miller said.

The waiter chose that moment to deliver our food. I forced a smile at him and said, "Thanks. It looks delicious." Pete and I both stared at Miller. He just stared at his food.

After the three of us were alone again, I said, "Let's get back to Snake. What happened with your illegal enterprise?"

"Things were going great for a while," Miller told us. "I was on the open road and the money was rolling in. What more could a guy want?"

"I'm guessing you got caught," Pete said.

Miller's eyes filled up. "You've got that right," he said. "Me and Snake. We both did a couple of years hard time. Not a good experience."

All I could think to say was, "I can't even begin to imagine."

"Don't try," Miller said. "It was as close to hell as I ever want to come." He stared off into the distance for a few moments, then continued,

"Funny thing, though. Doing time also changed my life for the better. Made me go straight when I got out. Got back to my old dream about coming to Nashville and singing my way to the top of the charts."

"How is that working out?" Pete asked.

"Slowly," Miller answered. "Very slowly. I wait tables up the street from here four days a week, mostly weekend afternoons. Also three nights a week, four if I'm lucky, I have a semi-regular gig in a club nearby. Audiences seem to like me well enough. I'm actually pretty good. The trouble is, so is everybody else in Nashville."

"I hope it works out well for you," I said to him, and meant it sincerely.

"Thanks." Miller swallowed the last of his burger, then added, "Funny thing, thinking about Snake. The first time I ever heard the guy's real name was the day we were in court. Malcolm Randall, the Third. Hell of a name for a crooked biker, don't you think? It's no wonder he went by Snake."

I wondered if as a child Snake had been called Randy.

Pete and I left Nashville late in the afternoon, in order to avoid the worst of the evening rush hour. I had hoped to stop at the famous Blue Bird Café on our way. It was well-known as the place where would-be performers actually had the chance to mingle with seasoned professionals and strut their stuff. The story was that many a career had its humble beginnings there. It sounded to me like a must-see place.

When I mentioned the Blue Bird to Gary Miller, he told us not to waste our time, that we didn't have a prayer of getting in the place without either a reservation or a several-hour wait in line. Oh well, maybe on my next trip to Nashville.

While Pete drove back to Hog Jaw, I telephoned Sheriff Snow with a request. Pete suggested I may be pushing my luck with the local authorities, asking a lot of them. I felt it was worth the risk. So far, Snow had been pleasant to deal with.

Today was no exception. Snow answered my call with a cheerful, "Well, howdy, Ms. Lynch. How is your case coming? Any progress?"

"That's actually why I'm calling you, Sheriff," I replied. "I'm hoping you can do a background check for me on a fellow named Malcolm Randall, the Third. Anything you can learn about him would be helpful."

"Malcom Randall," Snow replied. "The Third. Sure, I don't see why not. That name sounds kind of familiar to me. I'd be guessing this is related to the motel shooting."

"You'd be guessing correctly." I took a deep breath before hitting the sheriff with one other request. "I'm also wondering if I could get together with you or one of your deputies some time tomorrow to have you check my rental car for fingerprints. You don't need to come to the motel. I'm happy to bring it by your office."

Snow hesitated for a moment. "Tomorrow, huh? Is this important to you? Are these fingerprints somehow tied to your case?"

"Very," I told him.

"Care to tell me how?" he asked.

"Not just yet," I said. "So far it's just a hunch."

There was a brief pause as Snow apparently thought things over. Finally he said, "Well, sure then. I don't see why not. We usually let the State Police handle those things, but we do have a kit here. Might as well get some use out of it. I can have my deputy, Lucas Fowler, take care of that. Shall I have him call you in the morning to set something up?"

Whew! "That would be wonderful, Sheriff. Thank you much."

"I'm always happy to help," he replied, then added, "Do you think you might be on to something interesting?"

I told him, "I guess we'll find that out tomorrow."

I was ready to end the call when something else occurred to me. "Before you go, Sheriff, I do have one more question for you."

"Shoot," Snow said. "What's up?"

"It's about the Brave Hearts," I began.

"You mean that motorcycle gang? The old guys?"

"Right, other than that issue with the Indians have you ever had any trouble with them? Any complaints? Or run-ins?"

"Nope," he answered, "Can't say as I have. Why? What's up with them?"

"Actually nothing," I replied. "I'm just curious, that's all."

"Good thing," Snow replied. "A double-murder in Hog Jaw is all I care to handle at the moment. Let's not go looking for any more trouble."

Good plan.

Chapter 30

Wednesday morning

Deputy Fowler called while Pete and I were eating breakfast in the diner. "Morning, Ma'am," he greeted me. "The boss tells me you need to have your car checked for fingerprints."

"If it isn't too much trouble," I replied. Actually, I needed it no matter what, but it seldom hurt to be pleasant with the local authorities.

"I've got some time this morning," he said. "How does that work for you? Maybe in an hour or so. I'm heading to Jackson. I can stop by the Hog Jaw Motel on my way."

"That works just fine," I said. "See you then." That would give me time to get my thoughts organized before touching base with Peggy regarding what I had learned in Nashville.

Minnie dropped our bill off on her way to seat some people who had just come in the door. "Thanks, folks. Have a good day," she grumbled,

I gave her a great big smile as we headed for the door.

Pete's phone alerted him to a new text when we got back to our room. It was from Moira in his office. She was having some kind of crisis and needed his help. "It looks like I'm going to be tied up for a while," he said. "Moira's in over her head with something that needs to be addressed right away. Good luck with the fingerprints."

"No problem," I told him. "I think I'll try to work outside in the sunshine. See you later." With that, I dragged the desk chair from the room, grabbed my laptop and sat out on the sidewalk to wait for Deputy Fowler.

He was right on time.

"Howdy Ma'am," he said as he alighted from his cruiser. "Beautiful morning, isn't it?" He was short and thin, almost adolescent in appearance. And perhaps trying a bit too hard to grow a mustache. I wondered if this was his after-school job.

"Sure is," I replied. "I really appreciate your coming back out here for this. It's very helpful to my case."

"All part of the service," he smiled. "I'm on my way to Jackson this morning anyway, and Hog Jaw is right along the way. So what are we looking at here?"

"I need you to check for prints everywhere somebody would touch the front of the car when lifting and closing the hood," I told him.

"You've got it," he said as he headed to the front of the Mustang. "I won't be but a minute with this. I'll be out of your hair and on my way again before you know it." Fowler took some equipment out of his car and walked over to my rented Mustang to do his thing.

I was relieved to know he was heading to Jackson anyway. It made me feel a little less pushy, or perhaps less guilty, about asking for assistance once again. "Do you have any idea when we may get the results back on these prints?"

Fowler looked up at me from under the hood. "Pretty fast, Ma'am. Sheriff Snow has already asked the lab to put a rush on this."

Now that was interesting. "Was there any particular reason for that request?" I asked.

The deputy replied, "I'm not quite sure how to answer that. For whatever reason, the sheriff is all of a sudden pushing hard to close this case. I'm wondering if he's getting pressure from someone, somewhere. It's hard to tell with Snow sometimes. He tends to keep things to himself."

I walked a little closer to the Mustang and gave Fowler a look which was meant to say "Oh, really? Please tell me more."

Apparently the deputy received my unspoken message. "If you ask me, though, and strictly off the record, I'm thinking the hurry is all because of Lillie."

"Oh?" I responded, hoping that the other shoe was about to drop.

"Yeah. That's what I think. Emmet has always been protective of Lillie. Always watching out to be sure Jake was treating her right, making her happy. I think the sheriff never really got over their high school romance. And now he's probably trying to get Lillie paid the insurance money as soon as possible so she can get on with her life." He paused, closed the hood to the car, and added, "Or something like that. And, by the way, please don't repeat what I just told you, particularly to Sheriff Snow." He began to pack up his equipment.

"Not to worry," I assured him.

"Well, I guess I'll be going now. Somebody will be back in touch with you once your results are in."

My phone rang as I watched Deputy Fowler drive away. Peggy. I checked my watch. The office didn't open for another thirty minutes. She was early once again. She and I both often did our best work in the early part of the day. I went back into the motel room to speak with her.

"Please tell me you're coming home soon," she began.

"Are you saying that because you miss me? Or is there a problem I don't really want to hear about?" I held my breath as I waited for her response.

"Oh, damn!" she said. "I hate this."

It had to be bad news. Peggy seldom used expletives.

"It's Sam," she said, with a catch in her voice.

I sank onto the bed.

"Don't worry. He's OK now," Peggy hurried to add. "At least he's going to be."

I let out the breath I'd been holding. "What happened?"

"He got out," she began. "I don't know for sure how. I'm always so careful about locking the gate. He and I were in the back yard playing ball before dinner. I ran into the house for just a quick minute. To see if the oven was hot yet. When I went back outside, the gate was open and Sam was gone."

Peggy paused to catch her breath.

I waited impatiently for her to continue. When she didn't, I asked, "Do you have any idea how the gate got open?"

"An idea, yes. But nothing I can prove. My best guess is that nasty little brat from across the street let Sam out. Honestly, I can't believe how often that kid is out running free. I don't think his parents ever watch him."

I tried to hurry her story along. "So you found Sam pretty quickly, right?"

"Sort of," Peggy replied. "I started up the street, calling his name. When I reached the wooded area at the end of the road, I heard a whimper. Sure enough, Sam was there in the woods." She hesitated a bit too long, as if she didn't want to tell me the rest.

"And?"

"And his front left paw was caught in a trap."

"A trap!?" I exclaimed. "What kind of trap?"

"The kind you might try to catch a bear in," she said. "Only smaller, like for a rabbit. Anyway, I managed to get Sam free, carried him to the car and rushed him to the vet. He's there now. All fixed up. They're going to keep him overnight tonight, mainly to keep him as still as possible for a while. I'll pick him up sometime tomorrow. And update you on his condition right away."

As distressing as that was, I did my best to convince myself it could have been worse. I'd deal with the issue of the trap—and local ordinances—when I got home. I was pretty sure that sort of thing wasn't exactly legal in the Boston suburbs.

"So, everything's all right here," Peggy said. "Now tell me, what's happening out there in the back of beyond?"

I laughed. "Aka the ass end of nowhere." I filled her in on the latest developments with the case, then asked her if she or Tiffany could do a background check on Malcolm Randall, the Third. "And what about you?" I asked. "Anything of interest in your life? Or at the office?"

"Status quo on both," she told me. "George is out of the office for a couple of days. Nobody cares, let alone misses him. Nothing else of interest for the moment. I'll keep you up-to-date as needed."

We chatted and gossiped for a few minutes. Then I went back outside and sat in the sun for a while to work out what I wanted to ask Mr. Edwin Tuttle at Armstrong in the afternoon.

Chapter 31

Wednesday afternoon

I had hoped that Pete would accompany me to Armstrong Industries that afternoon. Such was not the case. The issue in his office Moira had called on turned out to be a big deal. He hoped he'd be able to resolve it remotely but expected it to take most of the day. I wished him luck and forged on alone.

I pulled into the parking lot at Armstrong Industries twenty minutes before my scheduled appointment with the head honcho Edwin Tuttle. I had done an extensive search on the man before leaving Hog Jaw. And learned very little. The man had no Facebook presence—not even on the Armstrong page. And nothing of any consequence per Google—a few individuals with that name, but the ages and/or locations didn't fit. The man almost didn't seem to exist except for a brief bio on the Armstrong website. Pretty much all I knew for sure was that he was ex-military, with no details at all on how long or where he had served. Either there was nothing interesting in Tuttle's past or somebody preferred to keep whatever it was quiet.

As I stepped out of my car, a male voice called out, "Hey, Ms. Lynch. Good afternoon!"

I looked across the parking lot and saw Sheriff Snow heading my way.

"Sheriff, hello," I said. "How nice to run into you." *And what in the world are you doing here?*

"Always a pleasure," he said, reaching out to shake my hand. "I hope things went well with Deputy Fowler this morning."

"Absolutely," I assured him. "The results of the fingerprints on my car could prove interesting."

He raised his eyebrows. "Care to tell me why?"

"Not just yet," I told him. "It's still just a wild guess at this point."

"If you say so," he replied with a slight frown. "So what brings you to Armstrong Industries this afternoon? Are you thinking they're somehow connected to your case?" The look on his face suggested he doubted any connection.

"Just covering all bases," I said. "Probably nothing of interest. But what about you? Why are you here?"

Snow frowned. "No big deal, really. Just a few minor thefts. A couple of Armstrong employees have had items taken from their cars recently—a cell phone, a portable GPS, a couple of empty backpacks. My best guess is that the local teenagers have been cutting through the parking lot on their way to beer parties in the woods. There has also been some minor vandalism to a couple of vehicles, mostly nothing more than a few scratches. I'm not sure what I can do about any of it, maybe not even sure I want to do anything."

I digested this information for a few moments. I couldn't help but wonder if the sheriff's office was too busy with other cases of local crime to ride herd on the local teens. Or perhaps they simply didn't consider this all that important. I chose not to comment. Now was not the time. The issue was not my business.

"There's always something with these folks," Snow continued. "Nuisance complaints for the most part. They complain about hikers cutting across their property. Or trash left in the surrounding woods, which I'm not even sure are Armstrong property. Then there's too much noise from weekend hikers. Most of it is just a perfect waste of time. I'm beginning to wish the town had never allowed them to build here."

"Any idea why they did?" I had to ask.

"We needed the tax revenue," the sheriff said. "Small rural towns like Hog Jaw need every penny they can get, mostly just to maintain the roads." He paused for a moment, then added, "And to pay our salaries. I suppose I shouldn't complain about it, although it seems to give these folks the impression they can monopolize our time. Every once in a while, we do have other concerns, other problems to deal with. Bad things do crop up sometimes, you know, even in a quiet place like Hog Jaw. Like the shooting at the motel. Things like that. More and more things like that these days." He frowned mightily.

I checked my watch. "I need to go in now. It's almost time for my appointment with Edwin Tuttle."

Snow nodded. I'll get back to you when I get the results of those fingerprints."

I walked across the parking lot to the door of Armstrong Industries.

A middle-aged man wearing chinos, a blue shirt with the Armstrong logo on it and a mean look on his face met me at the front door. He was over 6 feet tall, all of it solid muscle. Under certain circumstances, I guessed he could be intimidating. "Ms. Lynch," he said. It was a statement, not a question. "Follow me."

I did as instructed, even though he didn't say "please."

The interior of the building could only be described as stark. We walked down a long, narrow corridor past a couple of closed doors with the sound of machinery coming from them, passing nobody along the way.

At the end of the corridor, my guide knocked three times on a door labeled "Office". No mention of whose.

A male voice said, "Enter".

The air inside the office was dry and stuffy. The décor was bland and utilitarian—a gray metal desk with a state-of-the-art computer and two phones on it—one land line, one cell—three folding chairs, a few old metal file cabinets. A middle-aged man with a graying buzz cut wearing the official Armstrong uniform rose to greet us.

"That will be all, Jeffries. You may go. Please come in, Ms. Lynch. Have a seat."

Jeffries left. I sat.

"Thank you for agreeing to speak with me, Mr. Tuttle," I began. "I won't take up much of your time."

'You better not," Tuttle snapped at me. "I'm a busy man. I wouldn't have agreed to speak with you at all if that assistant of yours hadn't been so doggedly insistent. Pushy, really. You should have a talk with her about that. Anyway, as long as you're here, what is it you wish to discuss?"

Retrieving my phone from my purse, I said, "Do you mind if I tape this?"

"Actually I do mind," he snapped. "Please put that away."

"I'm sure you're aware of the recent double-shooting at the Hog Jaw Motel," I said as I dropped my phone back into my purse." Once again I was tempted to hit the record button as I did so, but decided against it. The look in Tuttle's eyes suggested it may not be a good idea.

"I heard something about a shooting," he grunted. "Didn't pay it much mind. We're busy here at Armstrong. We have important work to do here. Nobody has the time to waste following the goings-on in this god-forsaken backwater town."

Please, tell me how you really feel about the place. "I've seen Armstrong employees at the Hog Jaw Diner on several occasions," I told him.

He gave me a cold stare. "What of it? People have to eat someplace. And there aren't a lot of choices in this neck of the woods."

"I'd like to ask them a few questions," I said.

"About what?" His stare morphed from cold to downright frigid.

"The shooting. I need to speak with anybody who was in the diner around the time of the incident. I'm hoping that somebody overheard, or saw, something which may help my case."

"There's no point bothering my guys with any of that," he growled. "Folks here don't get involved with the locals."

Did that mean his "guys" weren't locals? "Do any of your employees come from around here?" I asked.

Tuttle shook his head. "You do know we manufacture bombs here, don't you? It's a highly sensitive business. It requires well-trained, highly-skilled workers."

I took that as a "no." "And where do you find such people?" I asked.

Tuttle rolled his eyes like I was some kind of a moron. "From the military, of course. Or actually ex-military. They have the training and experience needed to make this venture a success. And the good sense to do their jobs and mind their own business. Is there anything else you want to know?"

"What do your employees do in their spare time?"

That question earned me a hugely exaggerated shrug. "If there's no other pressing business, Ms. Lynch, I have work to do. Jeffries will see you out."

Right on cue, the door opened and Jeffries entered the room. "This way please."

I couldn't help but wonder if either Tuttle or Jeffries could see the steam coming out of my ears. I wasn't ready for a fight with the people at Armstrong, though. At least not yet. I nodded to Tuttle and followed Jeffries to the parking lot.

I sat in the car for a few minutes to get my head on straight and my anger under control.

Chapter 32

Later Wednesday afternoon

I experienced an unwieldy mixture of negative emotions as I drove away from Armstrong. Mostly I was furious at the way Tuttle had treated me. I took my frustration out on my rented Mustang, driving on the country roads almost as fast as my mind was racing.

Somehow, I arrived back at the motel with neither incident nor injury.

Several long, slow yoga breaths helped me to pull myself together. It was only mid-afternoon and I still had things that needed doing.

The first item on my list was to gas up the car. I pulled into Ike's service station hoping he'd be busy enough that he'd simply filled up my tank and go on about his business. I wasn't in the mood for idle chat. No such luck, there wasn't another vehicle in sight.

"Good afternoon, Ms. Lynch," Ike said. "Fill'er up?"

"Yes, please."

My phone beeped to announce an incoming text. Before I could read it, Ike appeared at my side. "Mind if I ask you a question?" he began.

It looked like that was about to happen whether I minded or not. I put down my phone. "What is it?"

He cleared his throat. "Well, you see, it's like this. You've been here for over a week now and Lillie still doesn't have Jake's insurance money. Doesn't seem right to me. Please tell me that she'll be getting paid sooner rather than later."

Forcing a smile, I replied, "I'm working on it, Ike. It shouldn't be long now."

The look on his face suggested he didn't believe me. The gas pump chose that moment to register full. "Hold that thought," Ike said as he dashed off to replace the nozzle and close up my gas cap. Before I could formulate a non-specific way to respond to his question, he was back at my door. I handed him my credit card without even asking the cost. And while he was off running the card, a semi pulled up to the diesel pump, effectively eliminating the need for any further conversation with Ike. Every once in a while, things did actually work in my favor.

I pulled into my usual spot in the motel lot, just outside my door. Before getting out, I grabbed my phone to look for new text messages. Big mistake. Only one item. It was from Mark, and it wasn't a friendly check-in or reminder. "Remember us?" it said. "We miss you at the office. Investigating this case is costing us more than we'll end up paying on it. Please check in right away and come home forthwith."

I wasn't up for dealing with Mark at the moment. I also wasn't quite sure what "forthwith" actually meant in my case. That provided a plausible excuse for postponing my response. I pocketed my phone and exited the car.

Then I groaned audibly as I saw Lillie's sister Noreen making a beeline for me across the parking lot.

She greeted me with a suspiciously phony smile. "Hello, Amy. I was hoping to run into you today."

The best I could do was to respond, "Hello, Noreen."

"Do you have a moment?" she asked. "I could use your help."

Did I have a choice? "Is there a problem?"

Noreen took in a large breath then let it out slowly. "It's Lillie. I know she's doing the best she can right now, but her best simply isn't good enough. She's great dealing with the customers, but doesn't have a head for business. Not at all. That was always Jake's job. I've been helping out as best I can, but that simply cannot continue. I have a life, too. I need to get back to it."

She paused and stared at me, as if to ensure I understood what she was saying.

I chose to bite my tongue and bide my time.

"Lillie needs to hire an assistant," Noreen continued. "At least part-time."

"That sounds like a good idea," I said. I had an idea where the conversation was going, but waited for Noreen to drop the other shoe.

"That means she needs money," Noreen said. "And she needs it now. I just don't understand what's taking you so long."

"The circumstances surrounding Jake's death complicate the case in a number of ways," I told her. "I'm working with Sheriff Snow and other local authorities to help me resolve a few remaining questions. We're making progress. I should be able to get it all wrapped up soon."

I hoped she wouldn't press me to define "soon." Perhaps she thought it meant the same as "forthwith."

"I see," she frowned. "Would you be good enough to keep me posted?"

"Actually, Noreen, the contract with New England Casualty and Indemnity is with Lillie. Technically, I shouldn't be discussing it with you at all. I'm willing to bend the rules with that, but only just so far. As I said, we're making progress. It shouldn't be much longer." And that was that.

"We'll see about that," she spat at me as she walked away without saying goodbye.

I made a mad dash to the door of my room before anybody else showed up to question me.

Pete would make it better for me. He wouldn't grill me or complain. He'd just hold me tight and tell me everything would be all right. Or so I thought.

Boy was I ever wrong.

Pete was sitting on the bed, wrung out and weary looking and staring at nothing.

"What's wrong?" I asked him. "Are you all right?"

He struggled to smile in my direction. "Yeah, I guess so. But this afternoon has been a bitch-and-a-half."

"What happened? Was there a problem at the office?"

"A big one," he told me. "Real big. For a while there, I thought I was going to have to go home to straighten things out."

"Things?" I asked.

He shrugged. "A client went postal on Moira. He didn't like the way she was handling his issue. The details don't matter now. I won't bore you with them. I spoke with both of them, separately, then together, and somehow managed to calm things down. All's quiet now, thank goodness. I can deal with the fallout once I get back to the office. Which is something we need to talk about."

I gulped. He was beginning to sound like Mark. And it wasn't making me feel all warm and fuzzy. "How about we head over to the diner," I suggested, "and we talk about whatever we need to talk about over a glass of wine?"

And off we went.

The diner was virtually empty at that hour. Too late for lunch, too early for dinner. Minnie was in the back cooking up something that smelled delicious. Walt was puttering around, but after serving our cocktails, he made himself scarce washing windows, mostly from the outside.

I raised my wine glass and simply said "Cheers." Unsure of what exactly was on Pete's mind, I was hesitant to drink to anything in particular. I sat back and waited for him to take the lead.

Pete cleared his throat and hemmed and hawed for a good minute. He sampled his beer, then put the glass down and finally asked, "How long have we been here now?"

"Nine days," I said.

"Right," he continued. "And you're investigating a $500,000 life insurance policy where the subject is indeed deceased."

No question there. I held my tongue, curious to see where he was going.

"And said subject most likely did not die by his own hand?"

I nodded.

"That tells me the odds are pretty good here that you're going to end up authorizing a check to Lillie Taylor for half a million dollars then heading back home to Boston."

I nodded again, and bit my tongue.

"Can we do a cost-benefit analysis here?" Pete asked.

"No need to," I told him. "Mark is saying the same thing. And he's not wrong."

"Not wrong?" Pete said. "So that means he's right? And there's no logical reason why you shouldn't do exactly what I just said?"

"Yes," I responded. "And no."

Pete rubbed his temples with both hands as if trying to alleviate a headache. "Yes and no? I'm afraid you've lost me there."

"I can explain."

"Please do."

I sat back, swallowed a large gulp of wine and began, "There's more to life than business, whether it's life insurance or anything else. There's right and wrong, and life and death, and good and evil."

"I can't argue with that," Pete said, "but that doesn't exactly explain why you and I are still here."

I took in a massive breath and let it out ever-so-slowly. "There's something going on around here. And it isn't good."

Pete folded his hands on the table and leaned into me. "I'm listening. What, exactly, makes you believe that something allegedly untoward is going on?"

"It's a combination of things," I told him. "Things you've seen and things I've heard."

"Such as?" he asked.

"Such as an abundance of characters of all varieties. Almost too many visitors for a place as small as Hog Jaw. There is a surprising number of hikers. Where do they all come from? And what's the attraction here? Particularly during the week? What are the bikers doing in the woods when they should be on the open road? Not to mention how or why the bikers and hikers are on such friendly terms with each other. What are the truckers actually hauling? And how do the locals figure into this picture, if at all? Was Jake Taylor on to all of whatever is going on here? Or was he perhaps in on it?"

The thoughtful look on Pete's face told me I at least had his attention now.

I continued. "And when you add in the bomb factory and the fact that we know for sure that Snake is dealing drugs, it is enough to give you pause."

I paused, then looked Pete in the eyes and added, "And that's why we're still here."

That seemed to placate him for the moment.

The minute we returned to our room, Pete was back on the phone with Moira. No sooner did she answer when he stepped outside the room and closed the door behind him. Was there something he wanted to say that I shouldn't hear? I tuned into the evening news and out of whatever it was Pete was saying to Moira.

What seemed like forever later, he came back inside.

"That must be some big problem Moira's having," I said to him. "You've spent almost as much time today talking with her as you did with me." Unable to help myself, I added, "Are you sure it's all business you two are discussing?"

Big mistake. Pete virtually exploded at me. "What the hell do you mean by that? I told you that little dalliance was over and done with. It's all business and nothing but between the two of us now. And if you can't buy that, if you can't trust me, then I'm not sure what you and I are doing here." He stormed into the bathroom and slammed the door. I heard the shower running.

I hoped he was immersing himself in cold water to help him calm down. I sat down at my laptop and forced myself to work on updating my notes.

Eventually, Pete emerged from the bathroom and plopped into bed without a word. I pretended to continue working and hoped he'd calm down by morning.

Chapter 33

Thursday morning

Pete was still in a foul mood in the morning. He was distracted, almost grumpy. Definitely not in the mood to talk. I made the mistake of asking him what was wrong. His response was a simple "As if you didn't know." After that, I held my tongue, planning to wait it out and hope for the best. I hadn't slept well and was in no mood for a confrontation.

At the diner, Pete gulped down his eggs, finished his coffee, picked up the bill. He reached into his pocket for his wallet. "Oh, damn!" he moaned.

"Oh damn what?"

"My keys aren't here. They're always in this pocket. Always." A look of minor panic overtook him.

"Your keys? Really? Why in the world would you keep them in your pocket here? It's not as if you were going to be needing any of them in Tennessee. You should have left them in your suitcase." I probably shouldn't have added that last part. Still, at least we were talking now.

He gave me an "oh well, what can you do?" gesture with his hands. "What can I say? Just habit, I guess. I'm just used to having them in my left pocket. Pretty much all the time."

"Did you have them yesterday?" I asked. "Just in case you might need them in Nashville?" I regretted my sarcasm as soon as the words came out of my mouth. Sometimes, I just couldn't help myself.

Pete ignored my remark. He pursed his lips as he thought. Finally, he said, "Come to think of it, I don't remember seeing them yesterday either. But I wore a different pair of pants, so I figured they were still in my hiking pants, where they belong. Which means that they're probably back in the room."

We paid the bill, then left the diner and searched the room. No keys. We checked the car as well, just to be sure.

"Damn it all!" Pete cursed. "Where the hell else could they be?"

I sat on the bed and thought for a few moments. "I hate to mention this, but where else have you been lately?"

That brought a massive frown to his face. "The only other place I've been is Hog Jaw Mountain, when I met Shaman Thomas there the other day. I wonder if the damn keys fell out of my pocket somewhere along the trail."

"Good lord, Pete. I hope not. What are you going to do?"

He shrugged long and hard. "There's only one thing I can do. I've got to go up there and look for them. Now."

A hugely disgruntled Pete headed out on foot for Hog Jaw Mountain.

As I watched him walk away, my phone dinged to announce a new text. Mark. I decided to ignore it for the moment. Too many other things were fighting for my attention. There was so much I wanted, or needed, to do. Mark would have to wait.

First on my to-do list was checking in with Sheriff Snow about the prints on the Mustang. He picked up on the first ring and said, "Can't talk to you right now, Ms. Lynch. Got big things going on." Then he was gone.

I searched my phone for Deputy Fowler's number, then punched it in. It rang and rang. I was just about to give up and try again later when he answered. "Ms. Lynch, good morning. I'm glad you called."

That was encouraging. "Please tell me that means you have new for me."

Fowler laughed. "That's for darn sure. And I think you'll find it interesting."

"I'm all ears," I told him as I grabbed my notebook and a pen. "What's up?"

"The results are back for the prints on your car."

"That was fast."

He laughed again. "Snow told them to put a rush on it. For once, somebody actually listened to him."

"And what did they find?" I asked.

"The prints belong to a fellow named Malcolm Randall. The guy has quite a record. Some folks know him as Snake."

Son of a bitch! I was right.

"This guy's bad news," Fowler continued. "A career criminal, currently out on parole. He's wanted on suspicion of dealing drugs in and around Hog Jaw Mountain. There's an APB out on him now."

"That is good news," I said.

"What's your interest in him?" Fowler asked.

"It appears he may be somehow involved in my case as well. He has been spending a lot of time at the Hog Jaw Motel, and he's apparently quite friendly with Lillie. I'm not quite sure what their connection is, but I'm pretty sure there is one. Will you keep me posted?"

Fowler sighed. "You got it. Will do."

As soon as I ended the call, my phone dinged. It was Sheriff Snow. "Howdy," he said. "Sorry I couldn't talk earlier. Like I said, big goings on. Things have calmed down now, at least for the moment."

"What's happening?" I asked.

"Some hikers found a body at the top of Hog Jaw Mountain this morning. It was that Indian fellow, the medicine man who spends his time up there, doing whatever it is that medicine men do. He's been killed."

"Shaman Thomas?" I exclaimed. "Good grief! Killed? As in murdered? Are you sure? Do you know what happened?"

"All we know for sure so far is that his skull was bashed in," Snow told me. "By a rock. A big heavy rock. Looks like somebody came up from behind. Someone tall, based on the angle of the wound."

"Could you pull fingerprints off the rock?"

"We're working on that now. It's hard to wipe a rock clean of prints, you know." He paused, then added, "I just don't get it. Why would anybody want to kill the medicine man? He seemed like a decent enough guy. Never bothered anyone. Just did he thing."

I'm so sorry," I told Snow. "I met Thomas. I liked him. My boyfriend Pete ran into him on the mountain more than once. They spent some time together." I thought back to what Pete had told me about his encounters with the shaman. "Pete told me he seemed on edge, and very wary of something, or someone."

"I'd like to talk to Pete," the sheriff said.

"Are you still on the mountain?" I asked.

"Just left," he told me. "The body's on its way to Jackson. I'm following in my squad car."

"Pete left here for the mountain a short time ago," I told him. "It looks like you just missed him. When he gets back, I'll have him call you."

"I'd appreciate that. The other medicine man, the old guy from Pinson, is coming tomorrow to identify the body officially. Hopefully, he'll be able to bring it home with him then, as soon as the autopsy's done."

"I've met Shaman Joseph as well," I said. "Any chance Pete and I could join you for that? We'd both like to express our condolences to Shaman Joseph."

"I don't see why not," Snow replied. "Call me tomorrow to set it up."

"Will do." I ended the call more than a little shaken by what I had learned.

I knew I needed to deal with Mark, but wasn't quite up to it at the moment. I wanted to pull a Scarlett O'Hara and "think about that tomorrow." I texted Peggy to let her know my plan, such as it was.

The question now became to determine what was the best use of my time for the rest of the day.

I decided to begin with Lillie. After what I had heard from more than one witness, it appeared there was more to the woman than simply the grieving widow. It was time to learn what that was. And to determine if she had been open and honest with me so far or if she was just stringing me along.

Lillie was alone in the motel office. She looked up from the front desk when I entered.

"Good morning," she smiled. "What can I do for you today?"

Good opening line. "I'd like to ask you a few questions," I said.

"Sure. What's up?"

That's what I wanted to know. Rather than ease into things, I decided to try to shake her up a bit. It was often interesting to see what fell out when I did that. "Tell me about your relationship with Snake."

She gasped audibly and clenched her fists. "He's a regular guest here, has been for quite some time now. Same as the other bikers."

"And?" I prodded.

"And what?" she asked, with a tight, forced smile on her face.

"From what I've heard, and seen, you spend a good deal of time with the man."

She gulped. "I suppose you could say we're friends. I make it a point to develop friendly relations with all the regular guests. It's good for business."

I wasn't buying it. "Are you having an affair with him?"

Lillie banged on the counter and glared at me. "Absolutely not. I would never do that to Jake. Never."

I stood there silently and waited.

After an uncomfortable several moments, Lillie continued. "Jake rescued me nearly twenty years ago. He saved me from being shamed publicly. Gave me a life I could be proud of." She stopped and stared off into space, as if reliving an unpleasant memory.

Finally, I asked the obvious question, "How so?"

"I was pregnant and alone," Lillie said. "Didn't even know for sure who the father was. Jake married me. Made me respectable. Gave me a position I could be proud of in this god-forsaken town. Everything good in my life I owe to Jake."

"And what about your friendship with Snake?" I asked.

"Oh, that's just for fun, you know, a way to pass the time. Jake never was much on socializing. Snake was. It was never anything more than that. Jake understood. I know he did."

"What about Snake? Did he know it was just for fun?" I asked. I wasn't buying everything Lillie was telling me, but she certainly seemed to believe it.

She nodded wordlessly.

I had one last question, "Did you shoot Jake?"

"Absolutely not."

For some reason, I believed her.

"Do you know who did?" I continued.

She shook her head.

And there I was, back to square one.

Chapter 34

Thursday afternoon

I spent the afternoon avoiding dealing with Mark. I ignored his texts. Luckily, he didn't call. I almost considered shutting off the ringer on my phone, but decided against it because of Pete. He wasn't back yet, and I was unsure where to go next with my case. I decided to attack these two issues one at a time.

I began with the easy stuff, placing a call to Pete to ask if he had found his keys yet. The call went straight to voicemail. My guess was that he might be speaking with Moira, still dealing with the recent issue in the office, whatever it was. Or discussing whatever else it was that they were up to. I left a message.

Mark was next on the list. And I'd need Peggy to help me deal with that. I punched her number into my phone.

Peggy's usual cheery voice greeted me. "Hello to you. Please tell me you're calling to tell me that you've completed your investigation, authorized a check to the grieving widow, said farewell to beautiful downtown Hog Jaw and are now at the Nashville Airport waiting to board your flight back to Boston."

"Sorry, Peg. Not just yet," I told her.

"Hmmm. So perhaps you simply felt the need to pass the time of day chatting with me?"

Peggy had a way of making me laugh. "There is always that of course," I said, "but there is something more this time as well."

"So what can I do for you? I'm all ears and ready to help."

I took a long, slow breath, deciding how best to phrase my request, then said, "It's Mark. As I'm sure you know, he's rather unhappy with me at the moment and I want to avoid speaking with him for a while. Probably until at least tomorrow. Can you help me do that?"

Now it was Peggy's turn to laugh. "Until tomorrow, huh? That may be asking a lot. The man is focused on your case right now and is looking pretty unhappy."

"I know he's upset, Peg. But I just can't deal with him today. There are too many other things going on. Things that really need my attention. I just need to put Mark off for one more day. Can you find a way to distract him until then?"

I listened to the wheels turning in Peggy's head. After a few moments, she said, "How about this? We enlist Tiffany to help. Have her go to Mark to lodge a formal complaint against George. She's pretty much ready to do that anyhow. She could talk Mark's ears off for a while. She's good at that. And then Mark would be obliged to spend the rest of the day trying to make things right between Tiff and George. What do you think?"

Bingo! "I think that's ingenious," I said. "It should do the trick."

"I'll get right on it," she said, "after I ask you just one small thing, even though it's technically none of my business."

"I'll bite. Ask away."

"Is everything good between you and Pete?"

Good question. "I can't answer that right now. I hope so. He's been gone most of the day today. I'll know more when he gets back."

"Do I want to know the details?" Peggy asked.

"Not just yet. Maybe tomorrow," I told her. "In the meantime, thanks for the help with Mark. I'll fill you in on everything tomorrow."

I ended the call, then punched in Pete's number. Voicemail again. Was he still on the phone? Was he avoiding me, still angry about last evening? Was he simply otherwise occupied on Hog Jaw Mountain looking for his keys? Or maybe he ran into some of the sheriff's people there. I imagined it must be pretty busy on the mountain because of the shaman's murder. There were a number of possible scenarios to explain Pete's not answering his phone. I left another message and worked on convincing myself not to be concerned.

Turning to my laptop, I began to update my online notes, hoping that this process might spark a thought about something I hadn't yet explored. It took a few minutes for the process to kick in. When it did, I grabbed my phone and called Deputy Fowler.

"Ms. Lynch, hello again," Fowler said. "I'm just on my way back to the office from the scene of that Indian fellow's death on the mountain. What can I do for you?"

He'd been on the mountain? Hmmm. "Did you happen to see a fellow there named Pete? Pete Devereaux. He's my associate."

"Can't say that I did," the deputy responded. "I knew just about everybody who was there, or had at least seen them before. There wasn't anybody named Pete. Sorry."

I was sorry too. "I'm hoping you can do something for me," I began.

"If there's something you need and I can do it, I'd be more than happy to oblige," he said. "What's up?"

"Last Friday, a fellow named Graham from the State Police lab came out to the Hog Jaw Motel to take some additional fingerprints in room 8. I'm hoping you have the results by now."

"I'll check that out for you right when I get back to the office," he said.

"That would be great. And could you please check them against the prints for Malcolm Randall?" I asked.

"I don't see why not," Fowler told me. "I'll get on it right away."

"Wonderful. Thanks."

"No problem," he said. "I'll talk to you soon."

Soon came sooner than expected. I had barely returned to my notes when Deputy Fowler called back. "How did you know?" he asked.

Aha! Score one for me. "So the prints matched?"

"They sure did," he told me. "And that's gotta mean that Mr. Malcolm Randall, aka Snake, was in that motel room the night of the shootings. That makes the guy a person of interest, if not a suspect."

I broke into a large grin. "It does indeed, Deputy Fowler," I said. "And that fact means a lot to my case."

"That's great," he said. "We've already got him dead to rights on a variety of parole violations. Now we may be adding murder to that list."

"Thank you so much for your help," I said to him. "I won't take up any more of your time."

"It worked out well for both of us, Ma'am. And hope you find your friend Pete."

"I do too." I ended the call and sat there grinning to myself. Things were looking up for my case, big time. Now if I could just locate Pete, life would be good again.

I was about to try Pete's phone once more when mine rang. It was Moira from his office.

I made the decision not to take my annoyance with Pete out on her. Better to play nice, at least for now. Maybe that would help placate Pete, smooth things over. "Hello, Moira," I said. "How are you?"

"I'm all right. And I'm sorry to be a bother to you, but I need your help with something."

"You've got it," I told her. "What's up?"

"I need to speak with Pete. I have a question on something that can't wait. But I can't reach him. I've been calling his phone off and on all morning. It rings and rings and then goes to voicemail. Do you know where he is? Or why he isn't answering his phone?"

"I wish I did," I told her. "I've been having the same problem getting in touch with him. Please try not to worry yet. I'm sure everything is all right. As soon as I speak with him, I'll have him call you. How's that?"

"That's good," Moira said. "And I thank you for your help."

I ended the call feeling that perhaps I may have lied about being sure everything was all right. Pete had been gone and unreachable for too long. Something wasn't right. I could feel it in my bones.

I plopped down onto the bed, trying to quash my fears. It wasn't working so well. I asked myself why in hell Pete wasn't back. Blamed myself for upsetting him. I tried his cell again. Still no answer. Only voicemail. I wanted to believe that this was simply an issue of inadequate cell service on the mountain, but that hadn't been the case before. Why would it be a problem now? Was Pete still searching for his lost keys? Or was he off somewhere sulking? I called again and left another message. And struggled to convince myself that it was no big deal. He'd probably be back any minute now.

But then he wasn't.

Everything else going on in my life seemed trivial to me. I needed to locate Pete. Now. Nothing else mattered.

The afternoon dragged on slowly and painfully. I didn't accomplish anything, unable to concentrate on anything but Pete. I paced and fretted and stared at the phone.

Dinner time came and went. No Pete. It began to get dark. Still no Pete. I was beyond worried now. Had he taken a cab to the airport and headed home? Or had something happened to him on the mountain?

I called the sheriff's office to ask for help. The line rang busy. I left a message. Then I sat on the bed, put my head in my hands and cried.

When I didn't have any tears left, I called the sheriff's office again, this time to inform them that Pete was officially missing … and probably somewhere on Hog Jaw Mountain. Unfortunately, I had to leave a message again.

Chapter 35

I didn't exactly wake up the next morning, because I hadn't exactly slept. The one time I had actually started to doze, the nightmare of my fiancé Danny's death came back to haunt me. I had thought I was finally over that heart-wrenching time in my life. Boy was I ever wrong.

It was several years ago now. Danny and I had argued, not unlike Pete and I just had. I had started it back then as well. Apparently that was a pattern with me. Danny had been drinking. He took off in a huff, jumping in the car and speeding away. That was the last I saw of him. He went off the road and died in a ditch in the Florida Keys.

Now Pete had left angry with me as well. And he was missing. I couldn't shake the dread that he had met a fate not unlike Danny's. I didn't know if I could survive going through that heartbreak again. I needed to call Sheriff Snow but thought it best to be fully awake when I did so. And that meant caffeine. I threw on some clothes and headed over to the diner. It was late enough in the morning that most of the truckers would be gone. Things should be quiet. That was good. I really didn't feel like dealing with anybody, even just to say good morning. Because it wasn't even close to being a good morning.

Walt greeted me at the door. "Mornin', Ms. Lynch. Table for two?"

"It's only me today," I told him.

He had the courtesy not to ask why. "What can I get you?" he asked.

"Black coffee. And toast."

"Coming right up." He headed toward the kitchen.

I got a text message from Peggy while waiting for my breakfast to arrive. "Call me," it said. "Soon." Short and sweet, and a bit of a worry.

Soon was just vague enough that I decided Peggy could wait until I got back to the room. I didn't dally, though. Scarfed down my toast and gulped hot coffee, then was on my way.

I punched in Peggy's number on my way back to the room. "What's up?" I asked.

She sighed. "The usual, actually. It's just worse than usual today. Mark wants to speak with you ASAP. Knowing the mood he's in, I would most definitely advise against that. Better to give him a chance to calm down."

I went into my room and collapsed on the bed. "I can't deal with Mark right now," I told her. "Or anybody else either. I've got problems enough at the moment." Then I couldn't help myself, I sobbed into the phone, and couldn't stop.

Eventually I regained some small semblance of composure and filled Peggy in on what was happening.

"That's beyond horrible," she told me. "But keep in mind that none of it is your fault, and that Pete isn't Danny. Just do your best to remain calm. Maybe find something to distract yourself from thinking about it."

"Like what?" I sobbed.

"How about the case?" Peggy suggested. "Try to concentrate on that. Anything to keep your mind occupied until Pete is no longer missing."

I wasn't convinced, yet said to her, "I'll give it a try."

There was a loud knock on my door as I was ending the call. "Ms. Lynch! Are you in there?" a man's voice called out.

"Who is it" I asked.

"Deputy Fowler."

I dashed to open the door.

"Good morning," the deputy said. "Sorry I missed your call last night. We've already got a search party out looking for your friend Pete. But I think that when I tell you where I was and what I was doing when you called, you'll forgive me for not being there when you needed my help."

"Okay. So tell me please. Has something happened?"

Fowler nodded his head vigorously. "Sure has. We got Snake. Caught him in the act. No way he can plead not guilty. Not this time."

"Wow! That's great. You finally caught him selling drugs."

"Actually, he was buying, not selling. And there weren't any drugs involved for once," Fowler told me.

Huh? "Can you run that by me again?" I asked.

"He was making a purchase from an Armstrong employee."

I was almost afraid to ask. "What in the world was he buying from Armstrong? Please say it wasn't some kind of explosives."

"Would you believe a bomb?"

Of course it was. What else could it be? "Whatever for?" I asked, afraid to hear the answer.

Fowler frowned. "You know he's one of that biker group the Brave Hearts. Seems they're stocking up on weapons, getting ready for the revolution they claim is coming. Planning an assault on the Democratic convention this summer, or so I've heard. We've got Snake down at the station now. And that's where this all gets even more interesting."

"More interesting than trying to purchase bombs? Or starting a revolution," I asked, almost afraid to know what else might be going on.

"Well, as you know," Fowler said, "this isn't exactly the man's first offense. With the record this guy has, and the nature of the current offense, this time he'll be going away for a long time."

"Sounds like good news to me," I said. "I appreciate you letting me know."

Fowler blushed ever so slightly. "Well, you see, I thought you might like to have a crack at him too. You know, since his prints were found at the scene of the shooting. We haven't yet questioned him about that. I thought you might want to be in on that discussion."

My inner self rejoiced at how helpful the local authorities turned out to be. "I would love to have a chat with the man," I told him. "Let's go."

I rode with Deputy Fowler, the first time I remembered actually riding in a police car.

Deputy Young was in the station guarding Snake.

"I guess you can head on home now," Fowler said to Young. "Spend some time with that new baby of yours."

Young shook his head. "Wish I could. Emmet told me to stick around here, though. I'm not quite sure why."

I studied the scene before me. Snake's legs were chained to the chair and his hands were cuffed, yet he was playing checkers and chatting with the deputy. Southern hospitality at its finest. Snake looked up at me and said, "Morning, Ms. Lynch. How're you doing?"

"Somewhat better than you at the moment," I told him.

He shrugged. "What can you do? I'm guessing you might want to ask me something."

Officer Young turned his seat at the table over to me. Once seated, I looked Snake in the eyes and said, "Did you shoot Jake Taylor and Lou Bancroft?"

He nodded vigorously. "I'm afraid I did."

I looked over at Deputy Fowler, who looked back at me, quite pleased with himself. I turned back to Snake.

"Why?"

"Are you looking for the short answer or the long one?"

"Tell me everything, please," I replied as I grabbed my phone out of my purse. "Do you mind if I tape this?"

"Suit yourself."

I hit the record button and waited. Snake sat there saying nothing. I ran out of patience really quickly and said, "So what's the story? And please don't leave anything out."

Snake inhaled loudly and slowly, then began, "They knew what we were up to."

"We?" I asked.

"Me and the Brave Hearts," he said.

Apparently he wanted me to drag the information out of him one painful item at a time. "And what exactly did Jake and Lou know? What were you and the Brave Hearts up to?"

"Getting ready for the revolution. It's coming, you know. Sooner than you think. The Democratic convention's only a few months away now. That's where it'll start. We need to be prepared. And that means weapons. Lots of them."

"Weapons as in bombs?" I asked.

"Yeah. Right." He sat up a little straighter, as if proud of this fact. "And not only did we know just where to find bombs, the place was on our regular bike route. It took a while, but we eventually managed to get a couple of our guys hired there. The more clean-cut, ordinary looking ones, if you know what I mean. Armstrong doesn't hire any disreputable-looking types, no beards, no long hair. This was easier than trying to turn any of the existing employees."

I sat there aghast and waited for him to continue.

After a moment or two, he said, "Once these guys got established on the inside, all trained and whatnot, the two of them got down to work—for us, that is. They sold us bombs, small ones, one little piece at a time. Easier to sneak them out that way. Our guys pretended to be big hikers. Even parked at the bottom of the mountain and walked to work sometimes. That gave them an excuse to have a knapsack with them. Which they then used to spirit the bomb parts out and sell them to us."

That surprised me. "Sell? Are you telling me that the Brave Hearts *paid* your own people to do this?" I asked.

"Why not? They were the ones taking the biggest risk."

Something occurred to me. "Where did you get the money for this?"

"Selling drugs. Mostly weed. That was my job."

Of course. I should have figured that out. I took a minute to think over what I had just heard, then asked, "How did Jake and Lou fit into all of this?"

"They knew about it," Snake replied. "That trucker saw us in the woods a couple of times. Got an idea what we were up to. We actually caught the guy taking a picture one afternoon. We nailed him in the woods and tried to scare him into keeping quiet. He told us it was too late for that. He had already talked to Jake about it, told him what he'd seen. Said that he and Jake were planning to go to the sheriff. We couldn't let that happen."

"So you shot them both?"

"Right," he said to me as calmly as if we were discussing the weather.

How easily he talked about it all, as if it was simply part of life. "How did you get Lou to let you into his motel room?" I asked.

"Broke in while he was at the diner," Snake told me. "Easy as 1, 2, 3. He was running late that night. It was somewhere around 11:00 when he got back to his room from dinner. Who knew the diner was open that late? Anyway, I got him to phone the office to get Jake to come over. The rest was a no-brainer." He sat back and folded his hand-cuffed hands on his lap.

"How did you come to have Jake's gun?"

"That was easy. I asked Lillie about security at the motel one day and she showed me the damn thing."

I was quiet for a few moments, mentally digesting everything I had just heard. Finally, I said, "You do realize you just confessed to murder? Double murder?"

He shrugged. "Yeah. Sure looks that way."

"But why?"

He stared past me. His eyes teared up. Finally he said, "I've got cancer. Pancreatic. It's bad. And getting worse. The doc said I've only got a few months left. Seemed to me it might be better to spend that time in someplace safe and warm, someplace with three hots and a cot. Might as well be comfortable, if you see what I mean."

I understood what he was saying. I fought the urge to pity the guy. After all, he had committed a double murder. I got on with my interrogation. "What would you have done if Lillie had answered the phone that night?"

"Good question," he replied. "Guess I would have thought of something. Anyway, she didn't answer."

"How did Lillie fit into all this?"

"What do you mean?"

"Give me a break, Snake," I said. "I've seen the two of you together. You obviously had a thing going together. Did Lillie know about the killings? Was she in on it?"

Snake shook his head. "She didn't know. I was going to surprise her when it was done. Free her from that bastard Jake so she and I could run away together. And live it up with the insurance money for as long as we could."

"But that didn't happen," I pointed out, couldn't help myself.

Snake's eyes darkened. "The bitch blew me off, turned on me. Said she planned to spruce up the motel with the insurance money and run it all by herself. And the hell with me."

"Did she know you were the one who shot Jake and Lou? And that she could end up being charged as an accessory to murder?"

"No. Besides, she was too busy planning how she was going to spend all that money. All of a sudden, she was too good for the likes of me. That hurt bad."

As that information was sinking into my mind, Deputy Fowler's phone beeped. He checked the caller then stepped outside to answer it.

I had one final question for Snake. "I get why you're owning up to your part in all of this. Why are you implicating the other Brave Hearts as well?"

"Wasn't my idea," he shrugged. "It was our inside guys at Armstrong. Once they heard I'd been arrested, they fessed up real fast, probably thinking they could cut a deal. I'm screwed anyway. So I told the whole story. You know—share the wealth, share the blame. It's not like they're going to come after me for it. At the very least, they'll need to start the revolution without me.'"

Before I could react to that, Fowler burst back inside. "They found Pete," he shouted. "He's alive. Come on. Snow thought you'd want to be there once they rescue him."

"Rescue him from what?" I asked, grabbing my purse and heading for the door.

"I'll tell you on the way," Fowler answered.

Chapter 36

Friday, late morning

My second ride in a police car was far more exciting than the first, not to mention a little bit unnerving. Fowler drove up the country roads at breakneck speed with his siren blaring and his lights flashing.

I closed my eyes and worked on breathing regularly. "Okay," I said to Fowler. "Tell me about Pete. Tell me everything."

"Like I said," Fowler began, "he's alive. Seems he fell into some sort of sink hole or crevasse near the top of the mountain. Lord knows how. Snow said he got banged up a bit, but he is conscious and able to converse with them a little. A rescue team is on its way now to get him out of the hole. Snow says he's waiting for them at the bottom of the mountain, in the parking lot near the first hiking trail. We'll meet him there."

Conscious was a good thing. Conversing helped too. I was worried about the banged up part though. How bad was it? I was almost afraid to know. The ride seemed to take forever, even at our ungodly rate of speed.

Eventually we screeched to a stop in the parking lot. I jumped out to join Sheriff Snow. Fowler locked the squad car, then joined us.

"We can go up this route," Snow said, indicating the beginning of a hiking path. "It'll take a few minutes longer to get to the top this way, but it'll be safer. Some of the other trails are pretty steep."

A rescue team consisting of an ambulance, a hook and ladder truck and at least six burly firefighters and two EMTs arrived in a storm of dust. Snow had a few words with them pointed the way, then rejoined us. "We'll let them get a head start," he said. "Then you can follow me."

Eventually we all arrived at a spot near the top of the mountain. The scene there was one of controlled chaos. Everything was happening at once. Medics were carrying a stretcher toward what appeared to be a hole in the ground. Others were gathered around the hole, leaning in and shouting, assuring Pete that help was indeed on the way.

I began to run toward the hole. Snow held me back. "Hang on there, Ms. Lynch. Stand aside and let these guys do their job. I guarantee they all know what they're doing. They'll have your friend out before you know it."

I did my best to play assured and patient. I wasn't good at it. I froze in place and watched the rescue team work. Snow was right. They certainly seemed to know the drill.

Then all activity stopped. The men by the edge of the hole shook their heads in disbelief as they pulled the ladder back out. A fellow who appeared to be in charge came over to me and Snow. "Hole's deeper than we thought," he said. "Ladder isn't going to do it. Looks like we're going to need to use the rescue harness, and a *lot* of rope." The grim look on his face was not encouraging.

Sheriff Snow turned to face me and put his hands on my shoulders. "Now don't you worry. This is all going to work just fine. I've seen them do this with the harness more than once. Just try to relax."

I forced myself to believe him, but the tears streaming down my cheeks appeared to think otherwise. And trying to relax was definitely out of the question. I was almost afraid to look over toward the hole, also more afraid not to. I wiped my nose on my sleeve, bit my lower lip and stood there dead still watching the men do their thing.

The rescue team finally stopped fidgeting with the harness. "Okay," one of them said. "Here goes." They dropped a harness on a heavy rope down into the hole. Then, ever so slowly, the smallest of the rescuers lowered himself into the hole. The scene became silent as a tomb as the fellow in the harness slowly slid downward and out of sight.

What seemed like forever later, a voice from the hole announced, "Got him! He's all right. Stand by." We listened to a lot of muttering and shuffling around, punctuated by the occasional groan. "This is going to take a few more minutes," the voice from below reported. "There's not a lot of maneuvering room down here. Not to worry, though. We have it all under control."

There were a few more groans, and a lot more muttering. Finally we heard, "Okay, guys. We're ready. Pull us up. Gently and slowly, if you please."

I had a brief moment of panic when it occurred to me that the rope might give way. Snow read my mind and said, "Don't worry none, Ms. Lynch. The rope will hold. It always does."

That told me the rope had been used before—more than once. Now I had a new worry. I closed my eyes and tried to remember to breathe.

A deafening roar of applause interrupted my effort. Opening my eyes, I saw Pete emerge from the hole, strapped into the basket seat and barely conscious. But definitely alive.

The medics dashed in. "Okay, folks," one of them shouted. "Give us some room here." Everybody backed away. I watched as two men laid a stretcher on the ground. Pete was gently moved onto it. A medic with a fuzzy white mustache moved in and examined Pete. "All right," he announced, "Strap him in. Let's get this guy to the ER. Stat!"

Stat didn't sound so good to me. I marched over to the stretcher and said, "Please, just give me one minute here." I bent down over Pete and took his hand. "Hello, my friend," I said. "You're going to be just fine. I insist on it."

He gave me a tiny, crooked smile and said, "I love you, Ames," then closed his eyes and drifted off.

The medics pushed me aside and ever so slowly began making their way down the mountain to the waiting ambulance. Snow turned to me. "Care to join me in the squad car? I can get you to the ER in no time."

I squared my shoulder and sucked in a breath. "Indeed I do. Let's go," I told him as we began making our way down the mountain.

The ambulance beat us to the hospital, but not by much. We double parked just outside the Emergency Room entrance. Pete was already being examined when we entered the waiting room. They wouldn't let us see him, just told us to relax and said they'd keep us posted. That was frustrating but understandable. We did our best to settle ourselves in the waiting room to keep vigil. Relaxing wasn't an option. The orange plastic chairs only made it worse. I alternated between pacing around the waiting room and sitting next to Snow trying not to sniffle too loudly. At least there was a nearly full box of tissues nearby.

Snow spent the time texting on his phone and occasionally leaving the room to speak with someone. We didn't speak much, but his presence still helped to keep me calm.

After the best part of an hour, a doctor came to speak with us. She was young and skinny with frizzy brown hair. She looked exhausted. "You can see him now," she informed us. "but only for a moment. We've given him something for the pain. He needs to rest."

I resisted the urge to hug her. "How badly is he hurt?"

She consulted the chart she was holding. "His left ankle is broken. He has a concussion. We're not sure yet how bad. Other than that, it's just bruises and minor lacerations. It'll take a little time, but he's going to be fine. We're going to keep him for a night or two as a precautionary measure. Monitoring for brain hemorrhaging mostly." She gestured with her arm. "You can see him only for a few moments before we admit him. Please come this way."

Snow and I followed the doctor down a corridor and into a room. I ran to the bedside and took Pete's hand. "Hello, darlin'," I said. "The doctor tells us you're going to be all right."

His eyes opened briefly. "Hello, Ames, I'm so glad you're here. I need to tell you something. It's important …"

Whatever he needed to tell me was lost in a slur of drug induced sleepiness.

I kissed his forehead. "Sleep well, my friend. I'll see you tomorrow."

Chapter 37

Saturday morning

Tomorrow couldn't come soon enough. Sheriff Snow drove me back to the motel, stopping along the way to get me a sandwich and a bottle of wine. I drank the entire bottle and still didn't sleep so well. I felt like a dishrag in the morning.

Two cups of coffee at the diner revived me somewhat. Walt was kind enough not to ask too many questions. He seemed satisfied with "Pete took a fall and hurt his ankle." Walt gave me directions to the hospital in Jackson and off I went, wondering what it was Pete needed to tell me.

Pete was sitting up in bed when I arrived at the hospital. He sported a helmet-like bandage on his head. His left foot was in a cast and bulging out from under the sheets. He greeted me with a huge grin, "Morning, Ames. How're you doing?"

"More to the point," I answered, "how are you?"

"I've been better, but in the end this is really no big deal."

I let my gaze wander from his head to his foot. "Oh really? No big deal?"

He shrugged. "Ankle's broken, as you can see. That'll heal. Minor concussion. Got to be careful, take it easy for a few days. I'll be good as new before you know it."

I preferred to have the doctor's word on that. "Have you seen the doctor yet this morning?"

"Not yet," he shook his head. "The nurse said she'd be by early this afternoon. I'm guessing that means I won't be getting out of here today. Bummer." He scanned the room as if looking for something. "Do me a favor, Ames. Check the drawers. We need to find my pants."

"Whatever for? You're not thinking about getting dressed are you?"

"Nope," he said. "This johnny is rather comfy. I need you to check my pants pockets for my phone. It's got to be there."

I walked over and rummaged through the drawer. The phone was there, under his muddy shirt, and looking more than a bit banged up. "It's here," I told him. "Who do you need to call that's so important?"

"I need for you and the sheriff to check out a picture I took yesterday, right before I fell."

I handed him the phone and stared at him. "You took a picture? Of what?"

He struggled to sit up straighter in the bed. "Let's wait until the sheriff gets here. That way, I can tell you both at once."

"Sheriff Snow is coming?"

"Any time now. The nurse's aide called him for me before you got here."

That all sounded rather ominous to me. I sucked in a huge breath and sat by the bedside to wait for Snow to arrive. Pete closed his eyes. I held his hand.

After a while, a voice called out from the hallway "Hello? Anybody there?" I turned to see Sheriff Snow standing at the door.

Good morning, Sheriff," I said. "Please, come in. Take a seat." I offered him my chair then seated myself gingerly at the foot of Pete's bed.

"How's he doing?" Snow asked.

Pete's eyes shot open. "He's doing just fine, thanks for asking. And thanks for coming."

"Not a problem. What's up?"

Pete grinned from ear to ear and looked from Snow to me and back again. "You're never going to believe what I have to tell you."

Snow turned his phone on to record. I did the same.

"So there I was," Pete began, "searching the trail near the top of the mountain, looking for my lost keys. And not having any luck at all. At one point, I decided I might as well take a few pictures as long as I was there. It is a beautiful spot. I aimed my phone down the path and took a few random shots. That's when I saw them."

"Saw who?" Snow asked.

"There were two guys coming up the trail in my direction. They were arguing pretty loudly."

"Can you describe these fellows?" Snow asked.

Pete broke into a huge smile. "I can do better than that," he said. He searched on his phone for a moment, then held it up for us. "Here they are."

Snow and I enlarged the picture and studied the two men in it. They definitely looked like bikers. One had a long gray ponytail, a scruffy beard and a beer belly spilling out over his pants. I guessed he was average height. The other was taller and clean-shaven, with chin-length dark hair. He had a gold nose ring and pierced ears.

"Didn't they see you on the trail?" I asked Pete.

He shook his head. "I jumped behind a large bush. It hid me pretty well, but I could still hear what they were saying. It was actually hard not to. They were arguing loudly."

"Were you able to record them?" I asked.

"Sorry. No," he replied. "I was flustered, and too busy trying to be quiet and stay hidden. No way I wanted to mess with these guys."

I got what he was saying, but it was still a disappointment. "Could you tell what they were arguing about?" I asked.

"About what they had done with the body."

"Body?" Snow asked. "Whose?"

A sad look washed across Pete's face. "Shaman Thomas."

"How could you tell they were talking about him?" I asked.

"One of them said something about how they were well rid of that pain-in-the-ass medicine man. He had been getting in the way of their business long enough."

Snow stopped him there. "What business was that?"

Pete smiled. "I'll get to that in a minute. From what they said, they had left the shaman's body in the woods. As a warning. To let others know that they were serious. That this was their territory and everybody else needed to stay the hell away. One of them was insisting that they needed to go back and bury the shaman."

I interrupted Pete's narrative. "Stop right there for a moment, please. Are you telling us you heard all this and those fellows never knew you were there?"

"What can I say?" Pete said. "I held my breath a lot, and didn't move a muscle. And like I said, they were yelling at each other."

Snow let out a little half-laugh. "You did well. From what you heard, it seems we might have messed up their plans by finding the body. Now tell me about the business."

"Right. One of them began pissing and moaning that Snake wasn't coming through so well for them lately. I hoped he'd elaborate on that, but he didn't."

I stopped him there. "Just so I'm following correctly, so far we know that Snake was selling pot, probably to hikers, and these guys were using the money to buy something they needed. Did they say what?"

"Not exactly," Pete responded. "But they were buying it from some guys that they had working in Armstrong Industries, so I'm guessing it was some kind of explosives."

Snow nodded.

Pete continued. "They were really antsy about this, saying that they needed whatever it was soon, because the time was coming fast."

"The time for what?" Snow asked.

"They didn't say."

I interrupted here. "Snake told me they were planning an assault on the Democratic national convention this summer."

"That's mighty helpful to know," Snow commented.

Pete laughed. "And it gets even better. Because then the other two arrived."

"The other two? Who were they?" I asked.

"Had to be from Armstrong," Pete replied. "They were both wearing those shirts that seem to be the Armstrong uniform."

"Any distinguishing characteristics?" Snow asked.

Pete frowned. "They were both pretty clean-cut, like the Armstrong folks we've seen in the Hog Jaw Diner. Short hair. Khaki pants. One of them had a mustache, if that helps. I believe he's from the Boston area."

"What makes you say that?" Snow asked.

"His accent. It was a dead giveaway."

"What about the other?" I asked.

Pete gave that some thought. "The only thing I really noticed about him was his ring."

Snow made a note. "Ring? What about it?"

"It was a claddagh ring."

"Huh?" Snow asked.

I pulled up a picture of a ring on my phone and showed it to him. "It's like this. It's an Irish symbol of love or friendship."

"Well I'll be" was Snow's response. "Did you get a picture of these guys too?"

Pete frowned. "Sadly no. Because that's when I fell." He closed his eyes and shuddered as he remembered the incident. Finally he continued, "I wanted to back up to take a picture of the four of them together but I was still crouching behind a bush. I inched my way back a bit over some spongy soil. And I felt the ground give way. The next thing I knew, I was at the bottom of a good-sized hole. My foot was caught in a crack and my head hurt like hell. I checked the sides of the pit for something to grab onto, so I could haul myself up. No luck. But I could still hear them discussing business."

I couldn't resist saying, "Are you sure it was them? Or did the bump on your head cause you to be hearing voices?"

Pete ignored that.

Snow spoke up. "So tell us about the business they were discussing."

"Right. One of them said it was getting trickier to get the goods out. That Armstrong was watching them pretty closely. Another was pissing and moaning that Snake was slacking off lately. What they referred to as his 'revenues' from marijuana sales were down. Had been for a while. And how did Snake expect them to get what they needed without the necessary cash?"

Snow scratched his head. "So what I'm seeing here is maybe two separate businesses going on: one selling drugs and the other, funded by the pot revenue, buying explosives of some kind. Have I got that right?"

"Sounds right to me," Pete told him.

I agreed.

Snow studied his notes for a few moments. "Based on what you've just told me, it sure sounds like we've got enough to put out an APB on these bikers, and to pay a visit to Armstrong. With evidence like this, it should be a slam dunk."

"I'm happy to help," Pete told him.

"I've got everything you just told us on my phone," the sheriff said, "but it sure would help if you could be around for the trial for a positive ID."

"I'll see what I can do," Pete said. "Just let me know when."

Chapter 38

Saturday afternoon

I spent the day at Pete's bedside. We chatted off and on about nothing in particular. He dozed a lot. When he was sleeping, I emailed back and forth with Peggy, filling her in on the whole bizarre story. I was glad I'd thought to bring my laptop with me. It was so much easier to use than my phone when I had a lot to say. I always did far better with ten fingers than with two thumbs.

Peggy was both supportive of my situation and fascinated by the details of my Hog Jaw adventure. Then she filled me in on the latest gossip at the office. She sent a wonderful video of Sam wagging his tail and grinning at me. I sure did miss that dog! The afternoon wore on.

On Peggy's advice, I also sent a short email to Mark, letting him know that the case was virtually closed and I would be back in the office as soon as Pete was able to travel. No way he'd be heartless enough to expect me to desert Pete to get home a day or so earlier.

Mostly I just sat and held Pete's hand while he slept.

I napped for a while myself as well, trying to catch up on the sleep I'd missed the night before. I was awakened by a voice speaking with a southern accent. I opened my eyes to see a youngish woman with a blonde ponytail wearing a white doctor's coat.

"Hello," she said. "I'm Doctor Carson. Sorry to wake you."

"That's all right," I told her as I yawned.

"Are you his wife?" she asked.

Before I could answer, Pete replied, "Fiancée, actually.

"I see," the doctor replied.

I was glad someone did. I was too overtired to react to that statement, though, particularly after the last several months. We could deal with it later.

"So how's our patient doing today?" the doctor asked.

I had little patience for niceties at the moment. "You tell me."

The doctor spent several minutes checking Pete out. Finally she said, "Everything's looking good. The ankle will heal, though it'll take longer than you wish it would. The concussion is fairly mild. Rest and relative inactivity in the near future will resolve that. Just don't push things."

"Does that mean I can go home now?" Pete asked. "Or at least back to the motel?"

The doctor shook her head. "Sorry. One more night here will do you a world of good. Tomorrow will be soon enough."

"Morning?" Pete asked.

"If you wish," the doctor said. She turned to me. "Any time after ten would be fine."

Pete had another question: "Does that mean I'm okay to fly?"

The doctor scratched her head. "How long a flight are you looking at?"

"Two and a half hours," I told her. "Give or take a bit."

"Can you sleep on a plane?" she asked Pete.

"Like a baby."

"Let's hope so. Please keep in mind that air travel at this point could exacerbate your concussion symptoms, particularly your balance. Also, you should probably use a wheelchair at the airports. And no screen time. No alcohol."

"Gotcha."

I headed back to Hog Jaw shortly after the doctor left. I was badly in need of both hot food and sleep. And I didn't want to be driving through terra incognita after dark.

Once back in Hog Jaw, I parked the Mustang and went straight to the diner. Walt met me at the door with a question on his face.

"It's only me tonight," I told him. Then I launched into the abbreviated version of what had happened to Pete.

As he listened, Walt opened a bottle of sauvignon blanc, poured me a glass and left the bottle on the table. "It's on the house, and all yours," he said. "I'm guessing you could use it."

He was right about that.

After a hearty meal of Minnie's chicken pie and an entire bottle of wine, I went back to the room and made arrangements to fly to Boston Monday morning.

Then I phoned Mark. Normally I wouldn't call my boss at home, particularly on a weekend evening, but Mark was different. After all, he was married to my best friend, Nancy. As luck would have it, she answered the phone. I gave her a blow-by-blow description of the past few days, shedding more than a few tears as I did so.

Luckily, Nancy had put her phone on speaker so Mark could hear my tale of woe at the same time. I was pleased not to have to tell it all twice. "Good Lord, Amy," he said once I finished, "That's horrible. I'm so sorry."

"I guess the good news is that the case is closed," I told him. "I'll arrange for a check for Lillie right away."

"I can help with that," Mark said. "I'll get a check issued and mailed out special delivery first thing Monday morning." He paused for a moment, then added, "And speaking of Monday, don't even think about coming into the office. Take a few days to help Pete and to pull yourself together. Consider it vacation time, but on the house."

What more could I ask for?

Chapter 39

Sunday

Pete slept through the drive from the hospital to the motel, then most of the rest of the day. I used the time to update my notes, confirm Mark's request for a $500,000 check for Lillie ASAP and close out the claim officially.

After that, I paced around the room, then the parking lot, torturing myself wondering if my mother had been right all along—that there was something inherently wrong with me and I would never manage to make myself happy, let alone anybody else that I actually loved. That I somehow managed to turn every perfectly nice relationship into a toxic mess. Danny and Pete were prime examples of what I was unfortunately capable of. I needed to work on that—sooner rather than later.

After an hour or two of this pity party, I set about tying up loose ends in Hog Jaw.

I began with Lillie.

There were a few Brave Heart bikers in the office settling their bills before heading out for the day's ride. I guessed that they hadn't yet heard about Snake's arrest and confession. I stood aside and did my best to look sweet and innocent. It didn't work all that well. A few bikers gave me dirty looks on their way out the door.

Finally the last of them left and it was my turn. "Good morning, Lillie," I began. "I'd like to settle my bill. We'll be leaving early tomorrow morning."

"Does that mean my case is settled?"

"It does."

"And that I'll be receiving my insurance check soon?"

I smiled. "I spoke with my boss earlier. The check will be mailed tomorrow—special delivery. You should have it by afternoon. Also, I'd like to apologize for the amount of time it took to settle this claim. And thank you for your patience."

Lillie shrugged. "Whatever. Story of my life."

I was unsure how to respond to that. Instead I asked, "What will you do now? Do you have any plans?"

"It's time for me to get serious about running this place, making a success of it. I want to spruce it up a bit," she told me. "And look for ways to bring in more business, different business. Hopefully better business. I'm guessing I won't be seeing much of the Brave Hearts anymore."

"There are other bikers clubs," I said. "And hikers clubs as well. How about advertising to them? Maybe offer weekend group rates or something?"

"Already on it," she said. "Noreen is helping, researching local groups, hikers and bikers, helping me put a letter together. Her English is better than mine. I'm also looking for ways to ask the truckers to refer this place to others. You never know. It might work."

"I wish you all the best with that," I said. And meant it.

"Thanks," she said. "How's your husband doing?"

"He'll be fine. Just needs a little rest," I said. I didn't bother to correct her about the husband part. Something else occurred to me. "Would you like to join us for dinner tonight?" I asked. "Our treat. As a thank you for being so patient."

Lillie shook her head. "Can't. Noreen's out of town. There'd be nobody to man the desk. I really need to hire somebody to help with that, at least part time. Now that I'll be able to afford it. Thanks, though."

I took my leave of Lillie and headed back to the room to check on Pete. He was sleeping peacefully. I sat at the desk and phoned the airline, confirming our flight in the morning and requesting a wheelchair both in Nashville and in Boston. Then I texted Peggy, not wanting to intrude on her Sunday. I let her know I'd be back in the office on Tuesday, but could pick Sam up on Monday if she wanted. That was enough work for the day. I climbed into the bed, snuggled up next to Pete and fell into a deep, dreamless sleep.

The next time I opened my eyes, it was nearly 6:00 P.M. I'd slept most of the day away. I shook myself awake, then nudged Pete. "Hey, buddy, wake up. It's time for dinner."

He rolled over and moaned, but finally managed to rouse himself.

The diner was about half full. "Evening, folks," Walt greeted us. "It's good to see you doing better. I hear you had quite an ordeal," he said to Pete.

"Comes with the territory," Pete responded, whatever that meant.

Walt served us drinks. Minnie served us rolls. We ordered meat loaf and mashed potatoes.

"Howdy, folks," a voice greeted us. I turned to see Sheriff Snow standing there, accompanied by Shaman Joseph and a younger man who appeared to be Native American.

"Thought we'd stop by to see you off," Snow said. "And to thank you for your help in cleaning up the illegal activity on the mountain."

"And for befriending Thomas," Shaman Joseph added. "Such a tragic end for a promising young man."

"What will you do now?" I asked, "About the mound?"

The shaman smiled at the young man beside him. "My nephew Matthew is training to take over Thomas's responsibilities there. I am confident he will do us proud."

That was good to hear.

Minnie delivered our dinner, the sheriff and the shamans left and Pete and I dug into our food.

We devoured our meal in silence, topping it off with homemade apple pie, with ice cream. I'd cut calories another time.

Pete and I toasted each other. "Here's to the end of another adventure," he said. "May we have many more—although perhaps a little less lethal next time."

I drank to that, determined to find a way to make that happen.

About the Author

Like her heroine Amy Lynch, P.K. (Paula) Norton spent her career in the insurance industry. When she and her late husband Jack traveled throughout the U.S. and abroad, they entertained themselves by sitting in restaurants discussing interesting ways to kill people. As they plotted all manner of mysterious deaths and mayhem, the world of Amy Lynch was born. Paula's curiosity, passions and varied life adventures are an integral part of her series—interests such as Paris (Paula lived there off and on over the years), archaeology (Paula worked at the archaeological dig in Paris), spies (Paula is a card-carrying member of the Association of Former Intelligence Officers), Key West (Paula's favorite vacation spot), fencing (her husband Jack was an award-winning fencer) and cattle rustling (don't even ask why). *The Back of Beyond* is the seventh book in the Amy Lynch Investigation series.

When she is not plotting or writing, Paula is, well, plotting and writing. She is a member of Sisters in Crime, the Cape Cod Writers Association and the Association of Rhode Island Authors.

Paula resides in Easton, Massachusetts and Delray Beach, Florida.